The Green of the Spring

by

Peter Keating

Dedicated to the memory of Serjeant William Keating, Royal Artillery, and to all men from the Island of Ireland who fought in the Great War.

"Have you forgotten yet?...

Look up, and swear by the green of the spring that you'll never forget."

Siegfried Sassoon, *'Aftermath'.*

CHAPTER ONE

Belfast, 1ˢᵗ July, 2016

The boom of the Lambeg drum, like the beating heart of a giant.

Paddy, waving a small Union flag with one hand, the other gripping his Grandfather's tightly, looks up wide-eyed at the vast mural on the gable end of Beattie's shop. A gallant-looking officer of the Ulster Division beckons his men forwards towards the Schwaben Redoubt, advancing through a hailstorm of German shot and shell.

A large but somewhat subdued crowd of all ages lines the street, which is festooned with Union Jacks and various red, white and blue buntings, lending a slightly festive air to the otherwise solemn occasion. Paddy jumps a little as the Lambeg gives one last loud boom, then is silent. A whistle blows and the immaculately turned-out members of the East Belfast Somme Memorial Loyal Flute Band mark time for a few seconds before coming to a smart halt opposite the mural. There is some polite applause from the crowd before the whistle blows again and the band resumes its parade down the street to the strains of *Goodbye, Dolly Gray*. The Lambeg begins to boom again, pounded

3

on by a stocky young man with a crewcut, his face a mask of sweaty concentration. A vein at the side of his perspiring forehead bulges with effort, the muscles of his heavily-tattooed forearms rippling. At the head of the procession, a lean, athletic-looking drum major performs incredible acrobatic feats of baton-twirling. Paddy waves his flag and cheers enthusiastically as the drum major capers by, snatching the baton from the air with an impossible-looking catch. He looks up at his Grandfather and shouts to be heard above the noise of the band.

'Is it *really* a hundred years since the Battle of the Somme, Granda?' John Nelson, a wiry, still-handsome man in his early sixties, looks down lovingly at his eight-year-old Grandson, his smile belying the sadness in his eyes.

'Aye, wee mawn. A hundred years! Can ye believe it? Almost as old as yer Granda, eh? Ach, if only yer Da and yer Great Great Granda Tommy could see ye now! They'd be so proud of ye, so they would!'

Paddy beams. 'If my Da was still alive he'd be over there in France now, at the Somme, so he would! Can *I* go over there sometime, Granda? And see where Tommy's buried? And Ulster Tower?'

Ah, God. John has to clear the lump of emotion caught in his throat with a small cough before he is able to reply. He takes Paddy's hand and begins to lead him away from the crowd.

'That's better. I could barely hear meself think with all that blood and thunder! Aye, maybe we'll go over there next year Paddy, when ye're a bit bigger. But ye better start pushin' away yer pennies now though, wee mawn! C'mon, I'll bring ye back to yer Ma's now fer yer tae.'

Paddy regards his Grandfather gravely. 'Is it true that my Great Great Grand Uncle Billy was a Taig? Craig Jackson at school said he was. He says that all the Nelsons come from Taigs, really.'

John frowns, trying to appear stern, but Paddy's innocence forces an involuntary smile to escape him, making Paddy's face break into an impish grin.

'Paddy, Billy was a *Catholic*, and he was a brave man, so he was. Don't ye mind what any eejit at school says. I'll have a wee word with Craig's Da the next time I see him, so I will. Ye can be as proud of Billy as ye are of yer Great Great Grandfather Tommy. *I* am. Billy was Tommy's best friend, so he was, from the time they were both as young as ye are now. They started off boxin' together in the very same club that ye go to now. Billy's sister, Mary, was *my* Grandmother - *your* Great Great

5

Grandmother. She was a very brave lady too, so she was. She didn't have it easy after Tommy was killed on the Somme, I can tell ye. She was a young girl all alone with a wee babby - *my Da.* Tommy's family looked after Mary and my Da as best they could, but times were hard, so they were. She took Tommy's name and raised my Da to be the good man that he was.'

John's expression takes on a proud, faraway look for a moment as memories flash behind his tired grey eyes. A blink conveys him back to the present. 'Aye. She was some woman, right enough.'

Paddy's brows knit thoughtfully together again and he chews his lip. 'Where's *Afgannystan*, Granda? Is it farther away from Belfast than the Somme?'

The words pierce John's heart like a bayonet. *My poor son. He was such a good lad. Was it my fault? Was he punished for my sins? Ah, Jesus...*

John somehow manages to coax out a tired smile as he puts his arm around Paddy's shoulders and replies to him softly and kindly. 'Aye. It's the far side o' the world, wee mawn, so it is. Now, come on. I'll get ye a packet of wine gums in Beattie's before we go back to yer Ma's. Don't tell her I got them for ye or I'll be killed, so I will.'

He winks conspiratorially at Paddy. 'Ye know what she's like about ye eatin' sweets before yer tae.'

The bell on the door of Beattie's shop gives a reassuring little tinkle as Paddy and John venture into the cool, dark interior. They are met by the familiar mingled aromas of confectionery, tobacco, and potatoes, as well as traces of Mrs. Beattie's favourite perfume, lingering ghost-like here and there throughout the shop. The shopkeeper, Rab Beattie, a large, hearty-looking man with huge tattooed arms and the high complexion of someone who appreciates a fine whiskey, leans behind the counter.

' 'Bout ye, Jacky-boy! And will ye look at the size o' this young fella! What are ye feedin' him over there in Bluebell Avenue, eh?'

John smiles at one of the few men who would ever dare to call him Jacky-boy to his face. *God, how many miles did we walk together around the yards of The Crum and Long Kesh?*

'How are ye, Rab? How's Violet keepin'? And the girls?'

'Ach, sher Violet's grand thanks John, mate.'

Rab nods towards the door.

'She's out there somewhere, so she is, watchin' the parade. Our Janet's over in Canada now. She's gettin' married over in Toronto next year! Meself and the missus are lookin' forward to *that!*'

'Congrats, mate! That's great news, so it is!'

Rab beams at John, his complexion flushing further with fatherly pride. 'Ach thanks, mate. And our Katy's still teachin' over in London. She'll be comin' home for a few weeks now next Monday, so she will.' Rab winks at Paddy. 'Now, what can I do for ye two men?'

'A packet of wine gums please, Mr. Beattie', asks Paddy respectfully, producing a pound coin from his pocket and offering it up to Rab.

'Not a bother, wee mawn. Save yer pound, Paddy, they're on the house, son, so they are', Rab responds with a smile as he hands the sweets over, ruffling Paddy's unruly shock of red hair.

'Thank ye, Mr. Beattie', replies Paddy earnestly as he pockets the money and turns to look up excitedly at his Grandfather. 'We can put the pound towards going to the Somme next year now, Granda, like ye said!'

The two men exchange an amused look over Paddy's head.

'Ach, he's turnin' out a fine lad, so he is John. He's a credit to Helen and your Philip, so he is...' Rab looks down sadly for a moment. 'And he's a great credit to you too, mate. I hear he's gettin' handy now at the boxin' too, so he is. Well, if he can fight anythin' like his Da and his Granda, he'll be World Champion someday, isn't that right wee mawn?'

'Aye. I will, Mr. Beattie, and thanks again fer the wine gums', replies Paddy earnestly, prompting a hearty chuckle from Rab. 'Ach, sher yer grand, son. Tell yer Ma I was askin' fer her, won't ye?'

'I will, Mr. Beattie! 'Bye!', Paddy replies, popping a wine gum deftly into his mouth as he exits the shop with another merry tinkle.

'Look after yerself, mate. Love to Violet and the girls', says John, nodding as he exchanges a warm parting handshake with Rab. 'I'd better be gettin' the wee mawn home.'

A fine, misty drizzle begins to fall as John and Paddy stroll back towards Bluebell Avenue, the melody of the fifes and the boom of the Lambeg gradually fading behind them. Paddy chews contentedly on a wine gum as he walks side-by-side with his Grandfather in comfortable silence. Suddenly, the boy stops and looks up at John, certainty and determination written all over his small face. *God, I know that look so well. Ah, Philip, he's yer boy right enough, son.*

'I'm goin' tae be a soldier when I grow up, ye know, Granda! Just like me Da! And Tommy! And Billy!' John's heart is caught somewhere between sinking in despair and bursting with love and pride. 'Will ye tell me all about him again Granda? About Tommy? *And* Billy? *And* the Somme? *Please?*'

John sighs and lays a hand gently on the boy's shoulder. 'Of course I will, wee mawn', he tells Paddy kindly. 'I'll tell ye all I know.'

CHAPTER TWO

Belfast, 1916

The boom of the Lambeg drum, like the beating heart of a giant.

The stern countenances of Sir Edward Carson and Sir James Craig, nestled amidst a plethora of Union flags, stare uncompromisingly down at the street from the mural on the gable end of Beattie's shop and proclaim *WE WILL NOT HAVE HOME RULE!* The street, a riot of red, white and blue, is lined by cheering men, women and children, many waving small Union flags as the Band of the Ulster Volunteers marches proudly by, followed by a small detachment of troops on home leave from the 36th (Ulster) Division.

A burly bass drummer meanders across the street, pounding his Lambeg, as the snare drummers hammer out a tattoo and the fifes take up the air of *Goodbye, Dolly Gray*. The smiling soldiers of the Ulster Division carry their Lee-Enfields at shoulder arms as they march by four-abreast, their boots bulled to a mirror gloss, their buttons and buckles gleaming in the Spring sunshine.

Billy McNally, marching beside his friend Tommy Nelson, catches sight of his sister Mary in the front row of the crowd, waving and cheering excitedly as they approach her. He gives his friend a nudge. 'Look mate, it's Mary – over there!'

Tommy turns around and spots Mary, grinning helplessly as a slightly dreamy look comes over his face. Billy rolls his eyes, but can't help smiling in spite of himself. Tommy winks at Mary as he waves back to her and Mary, beaming, blows Tommy a kiss. Mary, her eyes fixed on Tommy, doesn't notice a young soldier marching in the rank behind him staring malevolently at her.

'Wee Fenian bitch!' Davey Patterson mutters bitterly as he passes by. The ill remark is overheard by a big veteran Serjeant marching beside him. Andy McNair, his bushy moustache bristling in disgust, stares hard at Davey, but the young soldier ignores Andy's glare, his gaze fixed straight ahead, boring malevolently into Billy McNally's back.

Tommy turns to his friend. 'Billy, mate, did I ever tell ye that yer sis is the bonniest lass in the whole o' Belfast?'

Billy sighs. 'Aye. Ye did. Only about a million fockin' times, Nelson.'

Tommy grins. 'We're goin' up Cavehill tomorrow fer a wee picnic, so we are!'

Billy, suddenly glum, regards his friend sullenly. 'Well, I hope it don't piss rain on ye.'

Tommy looks somewhat taken aback by Billy's uncharacteristic bad humour. 'Ach, yer a barrel o' laughs today aren't ye, Cheerful Charlie? What's the matter with ye?'

Billy lets out another long sigh, almost seeming to deflate as he does so. He manages a rueful smile. 'Ach, I'm sorry... Enjoy yer dander, mate, the two of ye. Don't be payin' any heed to me. I just can't get me mind off us shippin' out back to Seaford the day after, that's all.'

Tommy grins back mischievously at his friend. 'I'm sure Annie Frost could take yer mind off it, mate!'

Colour immediately floods Billy's face. 'Ah, fock off Tommy, will ye!'

The parade, heading towards town, eventually passes Mary and the rest of the people by, and the men of the Ulster Division march proudly onwards, to the whistle of the fife, the rattle of the snare, and the thundering beat of the Lambeg drum.

CHAPTER THREE

Belfast, 1916

In Belfast, Sunday is the Lord's Day – a day of rest, regardless of denomination. In the morning, all across the city, people put on their Sunday best, such as it may be, and prepare to attend their preferred Services, according to their lights. In the East of the city, the habitual industrial dawn chorus of hammering and riveting from the shipyard falls silent - the Sabbath Day being one of the few manifestations throughout the year of such a wondrous event.

The sunrise holds the promise of a beautiful day. All is peaceful in Bluebell Avenue, save for the odd cheeky chirp of a sparrow or cantankerous screech of a gull. At the end of the street, a massive ship under construction dominates the skyline. Its silent hulk, crisscrossed with scaffolding, towers above row after row of the redbrick terraces of East Belfast.

The familiar sound of his father, ever the early riser, moving about in the tiny kitchen downstairs wakes Tommy up. He takes a moment to stretch and come to, then jumps out of bed and flings back the curtains to reveal glorious sunshine. *Yes!*

Tommy smiles and looks up to heaven in delight. *'Thank Ye Lord!'* His younger brother, fifteen-year-old Dougie, begins to stir in the bed opposite with a weary groan.

'Close the curtains will ye, Tommy! It can't be time to get up yet, surely?'

Their father's call from downstairs immediately disabuses them both of such a foolish notion. 'Come *on*, will ye! Ye'll be late fer Service, so ye will!'

Their mother's irritated voice pipes up from the bedroom next door. 'Ach, leave them sleep will ye, George! Service isn't fer another two whole hours!'

Tommy grins at his younger brother. Iris Nelson could be a tough woman when she needed to be, and if something needed to be said then there was no better woman to say it, but she had a soft, kind heart for all that.

Mr. Nelson, unwilling to admit defeat, decides to change tack, switching from the stick to the carrot. 'Come on, I'm puttin' on the fry, so I am!'

Tommy and Dougie look at each other for a moment, then bellow down the stairs in unison, much to their mother's amusement.

'Comin' Da!'

Tommy. Across the avenue from the Nelson household, Mary McNally wakes up smiling in the small bedroom she shares with her two younger sisters, Siobhán and Deirdre. The two girls, sharing the bed opposite, remain sound asleep. Mary hears a floorboard give a small creak of protest from the room next door as Billy climbs quietly out of bed.

'Billy! Girls! Wake up, will ye! C'mon, ye'll be late fer Mass so ye will!'

Mr. McNally's roar from downstairs shatters the morning tranquillity, prompting a swift rebuke from his wife.

'Mick! Fer God's sake! Ye'd wake the dead so ye would! Take a seat and relax fer yerself will ye, and I'll get the tae.'

Mr. McNally mutters something unintelligible, but there is the unmistakeable scrape of a chair on the kitchen floor as he sits down.

Mary sighs and turns on her side. Lately, she feels an ever-growing distance between herself and her mother. Brigid McNally hasn't actually *said* anything about her daughter's relationship with Tommy as such, but Mary can almost feel her silent disapproval like a tangible barrier between them. Mary snuggles back down in the bed and pulls the blanket over her head. *Get up for Mass? I'd rather be with Tommy!* But perhaps it is best not to incur her father's displeasure, not to mention her mother's. Mary eventually swings her legs reluctantly out of bed and tiptoes over to the small wardrobe they all share, where her sisters are already sifting through their clothes in search of their Sunday finery.

The fresh Spring air is alive with birdsong. From the top of Cavehill, Tommy, again resplendent in his uniform, looks pensively down at the city of Belfast stretched silently out below them in a patchwork of red, grey, and green, with the sunlight glinting off the silver water of the lough beyond. He feels the tender touch of Mary's hand on his shoulder. Tommy turns around and takes Mary in his arms, gently brushing away a lock of her long fair hair from her smiling face.

'A penny fer them, Nelson?'

Tommy sighs. 'Ach, sher everything, love. The War. *Us...*'

Mary winks mischievously at him. 'I like the *"us"* part best, Tommy.'

Tommy smiles tenderly back at her. *I am the luckiest man in the whole, wide world.* 'So do I, darlin'.' He chews his lip thoughtfully, suddenly nervous. 'Mary, do ye love me?'

Mary gives a short, surprised laugh, leaning back slightly in Tommy's embrace. She looks half-questioningly into his sea-grey eyes, gently caressing his cheek. 'Of course I love ye, ye oul' eejit! Are ye feelin' alright?'

Tommy grins back at her, gently pulling Mary back closer to him. 'I've never been better, darlin'.' Suddenly, Tommy looks down at Mary's feet, a note of alarm in his voice.

'Wait! What's that on yer toe, love?'

Mary gasps with fright as Tommy drops to one knee. He deftly produces a small velvet-covered box from his pocket and places it on the toe of Mary's shoe. Mary, eyes wide, covers her mouth with her hands and stands staring at the box, speechless.

Tommy smiles tentatively up at her. 'Well, aren't ye goin' to open it?'

Mary, trembling, slowly bends down and picks up the box. She opens it carefully to reveal a small but exquisite solitaire diamond engagement ring.

'Oh! Oh, Tommy! Oh my *God!*'

'I love ye so much darlin'. I always have, and I always will. Mary, will ye marry me?'

A tear wells from the corner of Mary's eye and meanders slowly down her cheek. For a moment, she can only nod her head at Tommy as she sniffs and swipes the tear away with the back of her hand.

'Yes! *Yes*, Tommy! *Yes*, with *all* my heart!'

'Go on, try it on then will ye, so I can get up! Me knees are gettin' stiff down here, so they are!'

Mary giggles and playfully pushes Tommy over onto the grass. Tommy, laughing, gets to his feet and puts his arms around her. Mary tries on the ring and admires it, the small diamond sparkling prettily in the sunshine.

'Oh Tommy, it's *so* beautiful! How did ye manage to pick it out?'

'Ach, I'm full o' surprises, so I am!'

'Oh aye?'

'Aye.' Tommy leans slowly towards Mary, who closes her eyes in anticipation of his kiss. At first, his lips just brush briefly and gently against hers, then Mary responds passionately, and they kiss deeply and tenderly for a few moments.

Mary nestles her head into Tommy shoulder as he holds her close. 'What'll we say to our parents, Tommy?'

Tommy sighs. 'Aye... I've been thinkin' a lot about that so I have, love. I was thinkin' we should tell them alright, but I was also thinkin' that maybe we might go to America or Canada and make a fresh start of it together - *just us* - away from all the madness this side of the world. What do you think?'

Mary looks deeply and lovingly into Tommy's eyes. 'Oh Tommy, I think that's a lovely idea, and nothin' would please me more than for us to walk back through the front door of my house with me proudly wearin' this ring, but... Maybe... Let's wait a bit? I don't mean that in any bad way, love. I just don't know what Mam and Dad will say. *Especially* Mam.'

Tommy looks despondent. Mary offers him a smile of encouragement. 'Let me work on them - and I promise I'll wear your ring on a chain, Tommy, so I will. Right next to my heart.'

Tommy brightens. 'Aye. I think yer right, love. We'll think it out properly, so we will - the gettin' married, I mean. This madness in Europe can't last much longer, and I'll be home before ye know it. Then we'll tell 'em *all* together and I don't give a *damn* what anyone says!'

Tommy looks at Mary thoughtfully. 'I *would* like to tell Billy sometime though, love. Maybe not right away, but soon - when I think the time is right. Sher I'd want him to be Best Man, o' course!'

'What about Dougie?'

'Ach, he's too young, so he is.'

'I suppose... Well, I'm sure our secret will be safe with Billy now, don't you?' Mary smiles mischievously at Tommy, taking him by the hand and leading him back to where their picnic blanket lies spread out on the warm grass. 'Come over and sit beside me, Tommy.'

As they sit down together on the blanket, Mary draws Tommy gently but firmly to her, and their fervent passion gradually overcomes their initial, fumbling awkwardness. Mary lies back, sighing, as Tommy leans over and kisses her neck softly, before moving up again to meet her eager lips with his. Tommy looks deeply into her blue eyes full of the promises of youth, of love, of *life*.

'I love ye, Mary. I love ye *so* much.' A sweet whisper.

'I know ye do. I love ye too, Tommy... Now, come here to me, darlin'.'

Mary draws Tommy down close to her again and they kiss more passionately. The sky suddenly darkens, and a roll of thunder rumbles over the city towards them from across the lough. Tommy and Mary groan, then start to giggle as a heavy rain begins to fall, the deluge quickly soaking them to the skin. They shed their wet clothes and make love as the rain continues to pour down on them in bitter sheets, both oblivious now to everything except each other as they become one.

Their home leave is all too soon at an end, and the men of the Ulster Division begin their journey back to the War at the bustling Great Victoria Street Station. The Larne train, waiting with steam up at the platform, impatiently whistles its imminent departure.

As Billy bids farewell to his parents and his tearful sisters, Tommy shakes hands with his father, gives Dougie a hug and then a playful punch on the shoulder before turning pensively to his mother. He whispers softly to her as they embrace.

'Ma, if anything should happen to me, promise me ye'll look out for Mary. I love her, Ma, and I'm going to marry her one day.'

'Tommy, I – '

'Promise me, Ma. Please!'

Iris Nelson looks quizzically at her son, hearing the urgency in his voice, seeing the near-desperation in his eyes, and nods solemnly to him, swallowing hard.

'I promise, son.'

Tommy smiles and sighs his relief as he gives his mother a final squeeze. 'Thank ye, Ma. I love ye lots!'

He strides over to Mary, takes her by the hand and leads her a short distance away from the platform, seeking some semblance of privacy. They embrace, and share a long, passionate kiss.

'Goodbye Mary. I love ye so much, my darlin'. Promise me ye'll write to me soon, now.'

'I *will*, and I love ye too, Tommy - with all my heart! I want ye to have this.' She hands him a brand new, smiling photograph of herself. 'I want ye to put this in your breast pocket so I'll be right next to *your* heart.' Mary winks at him, tapping at her chest. 'Just like your ring is right next to mine.'

Tommy places Mary's photo carefully in his left breast pocket. 'I'll treasure it, darlin', so I will.'

The men begin to board the train as it emits another shrill whistle, and the Station Master yells *'ALL ABOARD!'*

'I have to go, love.'

'Oh, Tommy - Goodbye, Darlin', and God Bless!'

They kiss and share one final, quick embrace, and then he is gone, joining Billy in boarding the train just as it begins to chuff away from the platform. They wave to their loved ones, smiling from the door of the carriage as the train pulls out of the station. Tommy blows a kiss to Mary, and her hand flies to her mouth as if to catch it and blow a kiss back to him, but instead it remains glued to her mouth, choking back a sob. A horrible feeling of dread suddenly washes over her like a black wave.

Oh God, what if that was it? What if that's the last time I see him – either of them – again?

Mary puts a comforting arm around each of her weeping sisters as the train chuffs off into the distance. A tough-looking little red-haired boy standing beside them dressed in short pants and a flat cap continues to wave a little Union flag at the train until it vanishes from sight. He turns around cheerfully to the girls.

24

'Ach, don't be cryin' now girls, will ye! My brother Allan is on that train too and I know he'll be back soon. Sher they'll *all* be back tae Belfast before ye know it, so they will! The Hun is no match for our Ulster boys now, sher everyone knows that! Ye wait and see, our lads'll knock eleven colours o' shite out o' them, so they will!'

Looking at the boy's cheerful but earnest little freckled face, Mary doesn't know whether to laugh or cry.

Still standing in the door of the carriage, Tommy takes in a long, deep breath of dirty Belfast air, savouring it as if it were a breath of the purest air from a fresh summer meadow. Grinning, he gives Billy a hearty clap on the back.

'C'mon mate, let's go in and grab a seat, if we can. I've got some news for ye, so I have.'

Billy cocks an eyebrow askance at this friend. 'Oh aye?'

'*Aye*, and ye'll *need* to be sittin' down when I tell ye, so ye will!', Tommy replies with a wink.

CHAPTER FOUR

The SS Nova Scotia, June 1916

Their furlough already seems a distant memory, and their brief sojourn back at Seaford barracks in Sussex a mere blur of bayonet drills, bulling boots, square-bashing and fatigues. They cross from Newhaven to Boulogne aboard the *SS Nova Scotia*, a rustbucket of a Canadian steamer-turned-troopship. The old vessel sits low in the water, crammed as it is with men and *matériel* to feed the upcoming offensive on the Western Front.

Tommy and Billy stand on the crowded deck near the *Nova Scotia's* bows, leaning on the rail and looking towards the hazy, still-distant shoreline of France. The weather is unseasonably inclement, and the old ship pitches and rolls and heaves its way across the Channel in an accursed beam sea, much to the discomfort of many of the men, but much to the delight of the multitude of excited, screeching seagulls escorting the ship, ever ready to pounce on a tasty morsel of ejecta.

Davey Patterson stands greenly by himself at the rail a few yards away, doubling over every so often and voiding his stomach uncontrollably over the side. Beside him, a small, wiry soldier with a Canadian shoulder-flash looks down obliviously at the foaming grey-green swell below, smoking and periodically tugging distractedly at his moustache, lost in his own private contemplation.

Serjeant Andy McNair patrols the deck like some sort of nautical rooster, seemingly unaffected by the nauseating motion of the ship, stopping every now and then to have an encouraging word with the men of the Ulster Division. Tommy and Billy turn and attempt to come to attention as Andy strides cheerfully over to them.

' 'Bout ye, lads?'

'Sarn't!'

'Ach, sher stand easy will ye!' Andy nods in the direction of the French coast. 'It won't be long now, lads. Back to where the crack is, eh? How're ye gettin' on anyways? All okay?'

'Fine thank ye, Sarn't!'

'Aye, grand, Sarn't, thank ye!'

'Ah, that's grand so. I like tae see the men happy, so I do. Ye can't go into a scrap like this miserable, so ye can't.

Happy soldiers make good fighters! Well, I'll be seein' ye later so, lads. Carry on!'

Andy walks on up the deck to Davey and gives him a hearty clap on the back as Davey continues to retch over the side. 'Ach, ye'll be grand lad, so ye will! Isn't it amazin', though, how there's always carrot skins in there, even if ye've not touched a carrot in a week?' At this, Davey's stomach gives a particularly violent heave, and a seagull wheels, swoops down, and deftly catches Davey's vomitus in mid-air, flying away with a triumphant screech, its beady eyes bright with avarice.

'Dirty wee bugger!', Andy exclaims with a grimace. 'The gull I mean, lad, not *ye!* Ah well, 'tis too late to be getting yer sea legs now anyway, sher we're nearly there! Carry on so, lad!' Andy gives Davey another cheerful clap on the back, prompting another bitter, convulsive ejection. Grinning, Andy resumes his patrol down the deck of the *SS Nova Scotia.*

'That's Sarn't McNair', Tommy whispers to Billy. 'He was transferred to us not so long ago. They say he fought in the Boer War - *and* in the Dublin rebellion.'

'Oh aye? Seems a dacent enough sort, so he does.'

'Coffin nail, guys?'

'Eh?' Tommy and Billy turn to the diminutive Canadian soldier, who offers up his box of Player's Navy Cut, giving it an encouraging, tempting little shake at them.

'I said, would you like a smoke?' He nods towards the still-suffering Davey. 'It's workin' well at keepin' the smell o' puke at bay for me, anyways', he asserts with a weary grin.

'Thanks mate.' Tommy and Billy gratefully take a cigarette each, leaning over as the Canadian strikes a match in his slightly-trembling cupped hands and lights them up. The men shake hands.

'McKnight's the name. Bob McKnight. Sapper, Third Canadian Tunnelling Company.'

'Tommy Nelson.'

'Billy McNally.'

'Pleasure to meet you boys. You guys are with the Ulster Division, eh? My Grandaddy was from Coalisland, County Tyrone. He emigrated from Coalisland to an Island of Coal', the little man informs them enigmatically with a short laugh. Tommy and Billy give Bob a puzzled look. 'I'm from Nova Scotia', Bob offers by way of explanation. 'Same as this ship. I'm not sure if that's a good or a bad omen. I used to be a coalminer before the war.'

'Oh aye?', Billy replies enthusiastically. 'We worked in the shipyard in Belfast. Ye know, the crowd that built the Titanic? - Harland & Wolff.'

Bob nods, exhaling a lungful of smoke with an ominous-sounding, hacking cough. He spits a gob of thick, sinister-looking phlegm over the side that not even the most undiscerning of seagulls deign to venture near.

'What's it like down there?', Billy asks, spluttering a little himself as he takes a drag on his own coffin-nail.

Bob smiles ruefully. 'Down the coal mines over there, or down the explosive mines over here?'

'*Both*, mate.'

'Well, like I said, the coal minin' runs in the family - it's all I've ever known. But this minin' lark ain't for everyone, I tell ya. Me? I was born to it. I'm a long way from home, but you could almost say it's a home from home. One thing's for sure - it ain't healthy down there – in lots o' ways.' Bob flicks his cigarette butt into the roiling sea below, scattering a few vociferously protesting seagulls. 'I ought to give these things up for starters. I got a bad chest, ya see. From the coal dust. I used to lie awake at night when I was a kid, listenin' to my old man cough himself into an early grave. Then, one night, he just

30

stopped coughin', and that was it. Ma woke up beside him in the mornin' an' he was just as dead as he could be. He was thirty-nine years old.'

Billy and Tommy lower their eyes respectfully.

'Jaysus, that's awful, so it is.'

'Sorry to hear that, mate.'

'That's okay thanks, guys. The Black Lung does the job on a lot of us coalminers. I'll make sure it ain't gonna happen to *my* son, though. Me and my wife Trish, we got a little boy called Harry, see? He's six years old and smart as a whip. He could be a doctor or a teacher. Me and Trish'll see to that, insofar as we can. He ain't goin' down the mines like his old man or his Grandaddy. The Black Lung ain't gonna get him, that's for damn sure.'

'Good for you, mate!' Tommy gives Bob a good-natured clap on the shoulder in an attempt to lighten the mood a bit. He grinds his cigarette out on the deck with the heel of his boot. 'How's it going fer ye, over here?'

Bob offers them a conspiratorial smile and a wink. 'We're busy, put it that way.' He gives a chesty chuckle. 'Underminin' the enemy is almost as old as warfare itself, eh? But we're takin' things to a new level over here.' Bob lowers his voice to a strained whisper. 'We got nineteen mines dug along the entire length of the Somme sector, eleven smallish charges and eight biggies. The ones at Beaumont-Hamel and La Boisselle are fuckin' *huge*. This attack is goin' to kick off with one hell of a bang, boys. Still, it should give you fellas a bit of a leg up, so to speak, when you go in.'

Tommy whistles, impressed. Billy looks gravely at Bob. 'So, what's it like down there, in the tunnels? I honestly don't think I could do it, mate. I'm more the outdoors type, so I am.'

'Well son, I'm lucky that I'm small, cos so are the tunnels. Now, I've told you tunnelin' ain't for everyone and that's the truth. It's cold, cramped, dark, and wet down there. It's a different type of war than what's going on up topside. It's a *silent* war, a war of nerves. You wouldn't believe how well sound travels underground, and somebody is *always* listenin'. The Germans listen out for us, and we listen out for them. If the Huns locate our tunnel they might break through into it, and then there'll be a scrap at close quarters. That's why a pistol, a dagger, or even a sawn-off rifle comes in handy. Even a spade will do the job, if it comes to it. There ain't much room for fancy fightin' down there - just wham, bam, and thank you, ma'am!'

Bob gives a jittery little laugh. 'Then again, the Huns might *not* break into the tunnel - they might detonate a camouflet, collapsin' it instead. Then it's curtains for sure, I'm afraid. Even if the collapse don't kill ya, you'll almost certainly be suffocated by the fumes from the explosion.'

Bob pauses, nervously swiping the back of his hand across his lips before he continues. 'I've seen brave men, big men, guys who've faced the storm of artillery and machine gun fire up above literally *crushed* by fear underground - crushed by the awful, primal fear of being *buried alive*. Of course, I've seen men crushed down there for real, too. Suffocation is an occupational hazard, I'm afraid - and a constant one, at that. Tunnel collapses, flooding, gas - oh yeah, they'll all do the job on you, for sure.'

Tommy and Billy look at the little sapper, aghast. *'Gas?!'* Billy exclaims in horror.

'Yeah. But not the type you're thinkin' of – not the type that the Huns use. I'm talkin' about Carbon Monoxide. It builds up underground and it's a silent killer. That's why we bring birds down there, eh? Miner's friends! My canary was called Jimmy. I never did find out whether he was a boy or a girl, but I called him Jimmy anyways just the same.'

Tommy gives a small, uneasy laugh, exchanging a knowing look with Billy. *This lad has spent too much time underground. Too bloody much by half! His eyes are all a-glitter, so they are. Fever? Or approaching Madness?*

33

The diminutive Canadian sapper matches Tommy's chuckle with a nervous little chortle of his own, then continues his story undeterred. 'So, like I said, if Jimmy ain't looking too clever then it's time to go, eh? Otherwise, you'll nod off to sleep but you won't wake up – ever. When they find ya, *if* they find ya, you'll be just as peaceful and rosy-cheeked as if you went and nodded off on the job – but you'll be *stone fuckin' dead*. Well, I was lucky. I'm still here and poor Jimmy ain't. But the little guy did his job, eh? A real Canadian war hero. See? Even heroes can be yellow too, sometimes.'

Bob offers them another little nervous chuckle, followed by another great racking cough, the issue of which follows its predecessor into the sea. 'Man overboard!' Bob mutters distractedly to himself, his eyes following the glob's unmolested trajectory all the way down to the foam. He looks back at Tommy and Billy with a puzzled expression. 'What was I saying?'

'Ye were tellin' us about Jimmy the Canary, so ye were', Billy replies with a slightly uncertain grin, nervously shooting Tommy a sideways glance.

Bob nods vigorously, re-boarding his train of thought. 'Oh, yeah. I remember now. Jimmy. Gas. *Gas!* D'you know I fuckin' *hate* that word? See, I had a younger brother named Walt. Well, Walt was with the First Canadian Division at St. Julien last year. He was killed there in that big German gas attack. Him and two thousand other boys. Chlorine - simple, but effective. It attacks the eyes, nose, throat, and lungs. Ain't it hard to believe they've come up with some far worse shit since? Walt was only nineteen years old - just a *boy* for Christ's sake!'

Tommy shakes his head, speechless, beginning to feel sorry for the little Canadian sapper. *He's just an ordinary workin' Joe like us. He's a man who's been pushed too far, has given too much, and he's not got much more left to give.*

Billy discreetly produces a small hip flask and offers it to Bob. 'Get some o' this down ye, mate. It'll put hairs on yer chest and stop yer skin from crackin', so it will.'

The wiry little man, blinking back tears, gratefully accepts the whiskey, taking a long swig from the flask before swiping at his lips again with the back of a trembling hand. He gives a satisfied little gasp and hands the flask back to Billy, who takes a quick swig himself before passing it on to Tommy who obligingly completes the ritual by wetting his whistle before handing the flask back to its rightful owner.

'Thanks, guys. God, I needed that.' Bob lowers his voice conspiratorially again. 'I'll let you both in on a little secret. I'm headed back up to Flanders when we land back in France. Me, the Third Canadian Tunnelling Company, the First

Australian Tunnelling Company, and every other tunnel rat on the goddamned Western Front. *Our* job on the Somme is done. *Yours* is just beginnin'. Now, we got something big goin' on in Flanders. *Under* Flanders, to be more precise.'

Bob's eyes glitter with almost lunatic intensity, his voice becoming a low, urgent hiss. '*We're underminin' the entire Messines Ridge.* There's so many tunnels now through the blue clay under there that the whole ridge is like a giant lump of Swiss fuckin' cheese. At the end of each tunnel we're excavatin' big galleries. That's where we'll pack the explosives. *Lots* of 'em. You're talkin' about thirty-five tons of ammonal and guncotton on average. It's gonna be the best part of *four hundred and fifty tons* of explosives altogether. It'll make our little curtain-raiser on the Somme look like a fireworks display. It'll be the biggest man-made explosion in history! Christ, they might even hear it back in Nova Scotia! One thing's for sure, it'll be enough to blow the entire Messines Ridge and any Hun unlucky enough to be on it about halfways up to the fuckin' moon!'

Tommy and Billy gape at the little Canadian, incredulous. 'When?' is all Tommy can demand quietly. Suddenly, the light in Bob McKnight's eyes seems to fade, and his whole wiry little body seems to wilt a little.

'Next Summer, sometime. If there's anyone left alive by then.' He smiles bitterly as he offers Tommy and Billy his hand again. 'It sure has been nice meetin' you guys, but I gotta go now. Good luck to you both.'

'Good luck, mate.'

'Aye, best o' luck to ye, Bob.'

The men shake hands, then the little Canadian turns and begins to walk back down the deck towards the gangway. He pauses and turns around again briefly. 'Ya know, they say blowin' these mines under the Messines Ridge could make the big breakthrough, could shorten the War, eh? Ain't it worth *tryin'* for that reason alone? So, ya see for me, every foot of tunnel I dig means I feel like I'm a foot closer to home.'

The light in his blue eyes glitters feverishly once more. '*Home.*' He gives them a forlorn little wave and then he is gone, lost amongst the milling mass of khaki on the heaving deck of the *SS Nova Scotia*.

Just then, a tall, gangly young soldier bearing the red hand insignia of the Ulster Division on his uniform roughly shoulders Billy as he walks by, knocking him back against the rail. Tommy whirls around on the man angrily. 'What the fock?!'

Billy slowly turns, smiling unpleasantly, and faces his assailant. The exchange begins to attract the attention of other soldiers, including the ashen-faced Davey, as they sense trouble brewing, the prospect of a fight a welcome distraction from the monotonous and nauseating sea-crossing. Andy, having also heard the commotion, turns around and watches carefully to see what transpires.

Billy continues to smile coldly at the tall soldier. 'What's *yer* fockin' problem then, mate?'

The gangly young soldier's face contorts with animosity. 'I'm not yer mate, and *ye're* my problem ya wee Fenian fock, ye. Think ye're a fockin' hard mawn, do ye?'

Tommy takes a step forward and pokes a finger into the taller man's chest. 'Why don't ye do yerself a favour, ye fockin' lemon ye, and piss off before ye get hurt?'

The head-butt from the tall soldier catches Tommy by surprise, striking him right between the eyes and knocking him down, dazed. Tommy hits his head off the rail as he falls, and he lies stunned on the deck as Billy rushes to his aid.

'Tommy!'

Tommy begins to come around, his eyes re-focusing slowly on the concerned face of his friend. He attempts to reassure Billy, his voice weak.

'I'm alright, mate... I'm okay.' Suddenly, his eyes widen in alarm. *'Watch out!'*

Billy rolls sideways just in time to avoid the swinging boot of the lanky young soldier. He springs back to his feet and faces the taller man, cold fury in his eyes.

The gangly soldier rounds first on the helpless Tommy, addressing him with a hateful grimace. 'That'll shut yer fockin' traitor's gub for ye for a while, ya wee Taig-lovin' bastard!' He then turns contemptuously to Billy. 'Now it's yer turn, Taig-boy.'

The other soldiers on the deck begin to form an excited circle around the two protagonists, shouting encouragement at them both. Billy, his fists up, advances calmly towards the tall soldier, who raises his own hands and begins to circle Billy. The taller man tries a big right hand, but telegraphs it and is too slow. Billy, his timing perfect, steps low inside, and delivers his own crushing right hand to the lanky young soldier's solar plexus. Even as the wind *whooffs* out of the other man, Billy follows up like lightning with a left hook and a right uppercut which both strike the taller man's chin with bony *cracks*. The gangly young man's eyes roll back into his head and he is already unconscious before he hits the deck with a meaty thump.

The crowd of soldiers stands in awed silence. Andy McNair whistles appreciatively. Davey, disappointment and disgust written all over his ashen face, suddenly doubles over the rail again and resumes his helpless retching. The other soldiers, realising that the show is most definitely over, begin to disperse. Andy strides across the deck and stands irately over the tall young soldier, who although still stretched out on the deck, is gradually beginning to regain his senses.

'See me later, McEntaggart, ye lanky wee streak o' piss, ye. Now bugger off out of me sight!'

The young man gets up slowly and unsteadily, his face a study in shame and embarrassment, and replies to Andy with a sullen mutter. 'Aye, Sarn't McNair.' He slinks away sheepishly, rubbing his jaw.

Andy ambles over to Billy and Tommy, who has managed to pick himself up off the deck with a little assistance from his friend.

'That was pretty impressive, Rifleman McNally, if I may say so. Ye look like ye can handle yerself, so ye do. Do ye box?'

'Aye Sarn't, I've done a bit. But not lately though – until now, that is. Meself and Tommy've been boxin' together since we were weans, so we have.'

'Well, I've a proposition for ye, lad. It just so happens that I'm a wee bit of a boxin' fan meself! Now I'll let ye in on a little secret, the pair o' ye. We've received a challenge from the Royal Dublin Fusiliers, so we have. I'd take up the challenge meself, ye know, only me boxin' days are long behind me, as ye can see. The last time I stepped between the ropes the pair o' ye were still weans, so ye were. Now, the young lad they're puttin' up against us is supposed to be a right hard nut. I'm lookin' fer a fighter tae meet the challenge. One that actually might have a chance of baitin' this Dublin fella. What d'ye say, McNally, will ye fight for the Royal Irish? There'll be no gloves and no rounds, lad. A fight tae the finish. There's no purse, as such, but I've a handsome side bet on with the Dublin lad's mucker, a Serjeant I know named Boland. I'll split the winnin's with ye fifty-fifty. What d'ye say, lad, are ye game?'

Billy inclines his head towards his friend. 'What about Tommy? I'll want him in me corner, so I will.'

'What ye do out o' *yer* end is entirely up tae *ye*, lad.'

Billy looks Andy in the eye, chewing his lip thoughtfully. 'Sixty-forty to *us* and I'll do it... *Sarn't.*'

Andy gives a little chuckle of admiration. 'Yer a hard mawn McNally, right enough, so ye are! Done, lad! Leave it tae me. I'll sort out a venue in couple o' days. Just remember though, keep it quiet, lads. It's unofficial, and we don't want any fockin' Redcaps pokin' their snouts in. That'd be bad news fer the lot of us, so it would! We'll shake on it, so?'

Andy, grinning, spits in his palm and shakes hands in turn with Billy, then Tommy. The three men laugh as Davey discharges another gastric offering over the side of the *SS Nova Scotia*, much to the excitement and delight of the screeching gulls.

CHAPTER FIVE

Somme, June 1916

The smoky *estaminet* is abuzz with excitement, full of young soldiers from every corner of the British Empire, most of them in various stages of inebriation. Among the khaki-clad throng, boisterous Australians rub shoulders with circumspect Maoris, rowdy Canadians mix easily with their kilted kin from the Scottish Highlands, and Ulstermen banter with their Southern Irish comrades, their noisy but mostly good-natured repartee bemusing the men from the more far-flung outposts of Britannia.

The floor has been cleared and the crowd itself forms the makeshift boxing ring. Billy stands stripped to the waist, his hands expertly and tightly wrapped, while Tommy and Andy hover anxiously behind him, stealing nervous glances across the ring. Billy stares impassively at his opponent, also stripped to the waist. The young man's hands are bandaged less skilfully in a somewhat haphazard fashion, as if the concept of protecting one's hands is an unfamiliar one to him. He is a tough-looking, burly young Royal Dublin Fusilier with close-cropped fair hair who, despite his youth, sports the scars, the badly broken nose, and the cauliflower ears of a veteran street fighter.

Davey Patterson watches grim-faced from the crowd, sandwiched between a silent, hard-eyed Indian cavalryman and a tipsy Australian soldier wearing his slouch hat cocked back on his head at a jaunty angle, a jittering cigarette clinging precariously to his bottom lip.

Billy turns bemusedly to Andy. 'So much fer keepin' it quiet! There's half the bloody British Empire here!'

Tommy nods in agreement. 'Billy's right. This'll attract the Redcaps like flies to a pile of shite, so it will! We'll end up with fockin' field punishment number one *if we're lucky!*'

Andy cheerfully dismisses their concerns with a wave of one meaty paw. 'Ach, don't ye be worryin' yerselves boys, we'll not see any Mud Puppies around tonight - sher their Serjeant owes me a favour, so he does!'

Billy gives Andy a quizzical look. 'What the bloody hell are *Mud Puppies,* Sarn't?'

Andy rolls his eyes in exasperation. 'M.P.'s!... *Peelers* fer fock's sake, lad, *Peelers!'*

Tommy claps Billy on the shoulder. 'Look mate, just go out there and box this fella. Don't let him draw ye into a scrap. *Box* him and ye'll be grand. Then let's get the hell outta here before we get lifted!'

Billy takes a deep breath, holds it for a second, then exhales it in a long, slow sigh. 'Righto!'

An aging English Serjeant, a Londoner from the Post Office Rifles co-opted by Andy and Boland to referee the contest, steps into the middle of the ring and addresses the crowd. 'Roight, quoiet lads! Quoiet now, or you'll 'ave the Redcaps down 'ere! Now, oi've been awsked 'ere by both parties to referee this 'ere challenge match between the Royal Dublin Fusiliers and the Royal Oirish Roifles. And wot a mouth-watering match-up it is, pitting two foine foighters from the Emerald Oisle against each other! So, without further ado, introducing in this – ahem – *corner*, representing the Royal Oirish Roifles, the proide of East Belfast, Billy *'The Kid'* McNally!'

Billy raises his bandaged hand, acknowledging the cheers of the crowd. He turns to his seconds. 'Billy *'The Kid'* McNally? Is he makin' this shite up himself or did youse tell him to say all that?'

Tommy grins as he nods towards Andy. 'It was all *his* idea, mate.'

45

Andy looks over distractedly at the young Dublin fighter. 'Ach, yer full o' shite, Nelson, so ye are. Now, where the fock is Boland? Yer mawn over there looks like he's on his own, so he does.'

The Englishman extends his arm towards the Dubliner. 'And introducing in this corner, representing the Royal Dublin Fusiiers, from Dublin's fair city, *"Fancy"* Frank Finnegan!

Frank's big muscles ripple as he raises his hand to acknowledge the cheers of the crowd. For the first time, Billy looks slightly uncertain. 'He looks anythin' *but* fockin' fancy to me, lads.'

Andy gives Billy a reassuring pat on the back. 'Ach, ye'll be grand, lad. I'd say he's not exactly the sharpest knife in the drawer, by the looks. Like young Nelson says, box clever and ye'll do just fine, so ye will!'

The English Serjeant looks over quizzically at Frank. 'Where's your Second then, mate?'

'Serjeant Boland? He's bleedin' dead, so 'e is. Copped it from a whizz-bang not three hours ago, lads. Sher what could I do only keep goin'? Never backed ouve a scrap in me life yet, so I haven't. It's what 'e woulda wanted anyway, de pooer bugger.'

Andy slams his fist into his palm in fury. '*FOCK!* Boland's dead! There goes the fockin' side bet, lads!' He sighs resignedly. 'Ah well, we can hardly back out now, can we? Just fockin' bate him as quick as ye can will ye, McNally, and let's get the fock out of here!'

The old Londoner shakes his head sadly at Frank. 'Ah, roight sorry I am to 'ear that, mate.' He looks over towards Billy's corner. 'Gents, could I possibly impose upon you to provide a Second for this brave young Dublin gentleman so that we can get this 'ere bout underway?'

The Ulstermen look at each other uncertainly for a moment and after a brief hesitation, Andy sighs and steps forward. He strides over to Frank and gives his hand a tap with his fist. 'No problem, mate. I'll do yer corner for ye, so I will. The *Oul' Toughs* are okay in my book. Fought alongside some of ye in Dublin durin' the rebellion, ye know!'

'Thanks, mate. Appreciate it', the young Dublin Fusilier replies, somewhat ambiguously.

Andy dutifully takes up his station in the Dubliner's corner as the Englishman beckons the two fighters to the centre of the ring. Holding each other's stares, Billy and Frank approach one another, the English Serjeant standing between them. 'Awroight, you know the score, gents. Obey moy

47

commands at all toimes and keep it *reasonably* clean, eh? Now come in 'ere an' shake 'ands the both of you. Good luck and may the best man win!'

Billy extends his hand sportingly towards Frank, who ignores the gesture. Billy looks at the Royal Dublin Fusilier uncertainly. 'Good luck then, mate?'

'Ask me swiss, ya little Orange bollix ya. I'm goin' ta tear yer head off yer fuckin' shoulders!'

Andy bemusedly shakes his head as the crowd erupts with laughter. Billy grins at the young Dubliner. 'Ye've got yer colours *and* yer prediction all wrong, so ye have!'

Frank shakes his powerful arms to loosen up and show off his muscles. 'Get ready for a good oul-fashioned Dorset Street baitin' Billy-boy!'

The Englishman pushes the two men apart. 'Awroight, awroight, step back! Step back now, gents! Seconds out! Now, *toime!*'

The *estaminet* explodes afresh into a cacophony of noise as the soldiers roar their encouragement at the two fighters. Tommy cups his hands over his mouth in an attempt to be heard over the din. 'C'mon, Billy, get stuck into 'im, mate!'

Andy roars at his unlikely new *protégé* from the opposite side of the ring. 'Get yer hands up now, mate, and keep that big Dublin head movin', cos this boy can box, so he can!'

The two fighters circle each other warily, probing with jabs. Frank suddenly throws a big right hand, hoping to land an early knockout punch. Billy easily slips the punch and counters with two big thudding left hooks to Frank's body. Frank grunts in pain, and the crowd roars its approval. The Dubliner lurches forward and tries to hold Billy, much to the vociferous, jeering disapproval of the crowd, but the young Belfast man manages to push him away. Tommy and Andy continue to bellow instructions from opposite sides of the shifting, heaving ring of khaki.

'The body! Keep goin' tae the body Billy!'

'Watch those body shots, mate!'

Tommy laughs. 'It's a bit fockin' late for that now, Sarn't!'

Andy, grinning, pops his middle finger up at Tommy.

The two combatants circle each other warily again. Frank fires out a surprisingly fast double jab, catching Billy in the face, and follows up with a thumping big right to Billy's chin, knocking the Belfast man backwards, stunned and staggering.

The crowd roars lustily again, sensing blood. Frank tries to finish off the dazed Billy with a tremendous big right, but Billy just manages to sidestep it, and begins to regain his equilibrium. He fires out a quick double jab of his own at the still-advancing Dubliner, snapping his head back twice in quick succession. Undeterred however, Frank lurches forward again and throws a big left hook to Billy's head. Billy manages to duck under the punch and fire two massive right shovel hooks up into the grimacing Dubliner's ribcage. The thud of fists striking flesh resounds throughout the *estaminet*. The crowd howls as Frank, visibly hurt, staggers backwards, grunting in pain. Billy goes after him, feints a left hook and catches the awkwardly ducking Frank with a vicious, smacking right uppercut to the face, bursting the Dubliner's nose like a ripe tomato.

Billy follows up with a thumping straight right to Frank's belly. The battered and bloodied young Dubliner crumples to his knees as the air hisses out of him like a burst tyre. The crowd gives a huge, feral roar. The old English Serjeant ambles over to where frank kneels gasping for breath, and begins his count.

Davey, livid, roars at the Royal Dublin Fusilier. *'Get up off yer hole, Dublin boy! Get back in there an' lamp 'im!'*

The Australian soldier turns to Davey in annoyance. 'What the fuck, sport? I thought the Belfast lad was one of *your* mates?'

'He's no *mate* of mine, Digger.'

The Aussie shoots Davey a dirty look, but returns his attention to the ring, where Frank manages to get slowly to his feet on the count of eight, albeit still winded after Billy's crushing body shot.

Billy grins at his opponent. 'Had enough, have ye, big mawn?'

Frank, angry now, looks spent, but gamely raises his hands, ready to fight on. 'Never! I'll kill ya, ya little bastard!'

Andy roars at the young Dubliner. 'Don't lose the head now, mate! Keep calm! Get yer wind back, then hook off the jab!'

'Watch it Billy! don't let 'im get inside! Double jabs, mate! Double jabs!', retorts Tommy from the opposite side of the ring.

Bellowing like an enraged bull, Frank rushes Billy and throws a flurry of straight punches. Billy, caught napping by the speed of Frank's attack, raises his hands and covers up, moving his head evasively from side to side. The Dubliner's first left and right punches glance harmlessly enough off Billy's bandaged hands, but the next left opens his guard and the following big right smacks with sickening force into Billy's face, opening a cut over his right eye. Blood arcs into the roaring crowd from the impact, spattering the Australian soldier's face. The Aussie wipes at his face absentmindedly with the back of his hand. As Davey cheers wildly beside him, the jittering cigarette finally falls from the Aussie's bottom lip as he looks down open-mouthed at the blood on his fingers. 'Firkin' 'ell! This is *full-on*, this is!'

Hurt, Billy reels across the ring but somehow manages to stay on his feet, shaking his head to clear his senses. His chest heaving, Frank closes in for the knockout. Frank puts everything he has into a powerful one-two, but the bloodied, yet by now alert-again Belfast man slips deftly to his right and then his left, barely evading the Dubliner's knockout combination. Billy immediately counters with a tremendous left hook to Frank's ribs, the punch landing with a sickening crunch. Frank howls in pain, dropping his guard. Billy follows up with a devastating combination – a straight right, a left hook and another massive straight right that all thud squarely off Frank's chin. The Dublin fighter falls slowly and heavily to the floor like a felled tree.

The crowd erupts, but then gradually lapses into an awed silence as the mauled Royal Dublin Fusilier bravely tries to get to his feet once more and beat the count.

Tommy shouts at the young Dubliner. 'Stay down! Stay *down*, mate, before ye get hurt!'

Andy roars his agreement. 'Aye, he's right, mate! I think ye've had enough! C'mon, yer a game bugger, so y'are, but ye've lost this one, mate! I'm throwin' in the towel!'

Frank retorts angrily, his words beginning to slur as he desperately tries to regain the vertical. '*No!* Noh' yeh'!'

He just beats the count, clutching his side as he rises unsteadily from the floor like a newborn colt. The young Dublin fighter looks out on his feet, but nevertheless, he shambles bravely over towards Billy and, grimacing in pain, gamely pops out a tired-looking jab.

Billy, glancing questioningly at the English referee, has all the time in the world to duck the Dubliner's faltering blow. Determined to finish it now, he throws a big straight right that lands with a resounding *crack* on Frank's chin, flooring the brave fighter for the last time.

The Englishman waves off the contest and raises Billy's hand, to a roar of delighted approval from the crowd. The

53

Australian soldier flings his slouch hat high in the air, and Tommy rushes over to Billy, embracing him and raising his friend's hand in triumph. The old English Serjeant goes over to check on Frank, followed swiftly by Andy, who kneels over the half-conscious, groaning young fighter. 'He's okay. He'll live. He won't be doin' any boxin' again for a while, though. I think his ribs are busted, so they are.'

In the crowd, Davey shakes his head in disgust. 'Useless wee Dublin focker!'

The Aussie rounds on him angrily. 'Right, I've had just about enough of yer shit, ya gobby little prick ya! Try *this* on for size!' The Aussie's punch catches the young Ulsterman flush in the mouth, catapulting him back into a colossal, ill-tempered looking Maori soldier and knocking the New Zealander's lemon-squeezer hat onto the floor. The Kiwi calmly retrieves his hat, swats Davey away like a fly and strides over impassively to the Aussie, who gazes up at the Aotearoan giant resignedly.

'Super-Squeezer! *Oh, Shit!*'

The New Zealander grins broadly at the Aussie. '*Oh, Shit* is right, bro!' The last thing the Australian soldier remembers is the rapid approach towards his face of a fist roughly the size of a grizzly bear's paw. The Aussie's nose literally explodes on impact, and he is knocked flying into a raucous gaggle of men from the First South African Brigade, triggering a violent chain reaction in the *estaminet*. Bedlam breaks out as fists start flying and a mass brawl ensues.

A roar from a young Welsh Guardsman at the front door of the hall finally halts the carnage. *'Redcaps!* The M.P.'s are coming! About twenty of 'em, with batons drawn! Everyone out! Quick!'

Although still some way distant, the unmistakeable sound of the Provosts' shrill whistles can be heard approaching the *estaminet*, and the soldiers quickly begin to disperse. Davey picks himself gingerly up off the floor and shambles out the back door of the premises, alone.

Billy turns to Andy with a sardonic smile. 'I thought ye said we'd not see the Mud Puppies tonight, Sarn't?'

Andy shrugs, spreading his big hands and offering Billy a sheepish grin. 'Well, ye could hardly expect them tae ignore a fockin' *riot* now could ye, lad?'

Tommy hurries over to the defeated Royal Dublin Fusilier, who is still lying on the ground, clutching his ribs and groaning. 'C'mon youse! Help us get yer mawn here offside, quick! He's a game lad, so he is. He put up a bloody good fight tonight and I'll not leave him here at the mercy of those fockin' Peelers!'

Billy nods in agreement as he hurries over to assist his friend. 'Aye. He doesn't deserve to finish the night with a busted head to add to his busted nose and busted ribs. Let's get him over to his own lads and they can sort him out. C'mon, Sarn't, give us a hand, will ye?'

Andy takes a moment to consider the situation, then nods his assent. 'Righto then, lads! Easy with him now, though!'

The Ulstermen lift up the injured Dubliner carefully, but with as much haste as they dare manage. Wincing, Frank Finnegan regards each of them gratefully as they half-support, half-carry him out the back door of the *estaminet*. 'God bless yiz, lads, God bless yiz', he mutters through gasps of pain, and the young Royal Dublin Fusilier continues to shower benedictions upon them all the way into the balmy June night.

The old English Serjeant stands alone in the middle of the now empty, but totally wrecked *estaminet*, scratching his head and ignoring the remonstrations of the angry little proprietor wading towards him through the detritus, amongst which lies the still-moaning Australian soldier, his nose a flattened mess of blood and snot.

The Englishman begins to make his way unhurriedly towards the back door, muttering to himself as he hears a cacophony of whistles approach the front of the *estaminet.* 'Well, oi s'pose oi'd better make m'self scarce as well before oi gets m'self into more trouble with their lordships, but my 'eavens! Wot a bunch of mad Oirish bawstads!'

CHAPTER SIX

Belfast, June 1916

Sent home from the mill after feeling faint at work, Mary sits at the kitchen table, her face in her hands. Something is definitely amiss. *It should have been here by now.* Mary feels the first bitter seeds of panic begin to take root and sprout inside her. *Oh God, I CAN'T be!* But deep down, she is sure beyond doubt, and part of her even rejoices in the fact. *Our baby.* She imagines herself blissfully pushing a new perambulator through Central Park on a sunny Sunday morning in New York, her hair cut fashionably short in the American style, Tommy walking proudly by her side, tipping his hat to the fine ladies of Manhattan as they pass by, some of them even stopping to chat and admire her baby. *Their baby!*

Nausea suddenly overwhelms her, wrenching her all the way back to the harsh reality of a tiny kitchen in a tiny red-brick terraced house in East Belfast. Mary bolts out the back door, both hands firmly clamped over her mouth, and makes a brave dash for the outside privvy. She doesn't quite make it, her hands flying from her mouth and her gorge rising just as the privvy door is opened by her mother on the way out. Time seems to slow down to a nightmarish crawl, and Mary can only look on helplessly as she covers her mother from head to toe with a half-digested Ulster fry.

Mother and daughter face each other in shocked silence for a moment. Mary, caught somewhere between horror and hilarity, manages to stifle a mad urge to guffaw as runny pieces of sausage, bacon, black pudding, and fried egg drip down Brigid McNally's hair, face, and clothing, even spattering her shoes. *'Oh, God'* is all that Mary can finally manage.

'Hoor!' Her mother's heavy forehand slap shocks rather than actually hurts Mary, at first. Mary's hand flies instinctively to her face as she feels the reddening skin on her cheek begin to tingle, tighten and swell.

'Mammy, please! - '

'Get *out* of my house, ya wee *hoor*, ye!' A feral hiss. Brigid McNally pushes past her daughter, slamming the back door closed as she enters the house without a backwards glance. Mary stands there for a moment, crying silent tears of shame, hurt, and anger. Then, she takes in a long, shaky breath, gathers her courage, and follows her mother back into the house.

Mary hears her mother's muffled sobs coming from her parents' bedroom as she slowly climbs the stairs. *Thank God it's Saturday, and the girls are over playing at the Donnelly's.* She goes to her room and closes the door quietly. She takes a pad of letter paper and a pencil from the chest of drawers, but as she begins to write a note to her younger sisters, the sadness threatens to overwhelm her. *Oh God, what do I tell them? They are probably old enough now to read between the lines anyway. One way or the other they will be heartbroken.* Mary stifles a sob as she writes:

My Dearest Siobhán & Deirdre,

I'm sorry, but Mam and I had a big fight and I have to leave home for a while. It's all to do with Tommy and I, I'm afraid. Please don't worry about me, I'll be fine. I'll talk to Daddy and I'm sure he will be able to make it all blow over. I'll write again soon. Look after one another, and please remember me in your prayers, as I will you.

Your loving sister,

Mary.

With a sniff, Mary folds the note and places it on the pillow of the girls' bed. *What a mess! Oh Daddy, if only you had been here!*

But would her father's presence *really* have made any difference, she wonders? Possibly not. Mary has always been the apple of her father's eye, and she has always sensed a special bond between them that she feels is lacking in her relationship with her mother. Mick McNally is a big, quiet, man – gentle even, in his own way, but ever inclined to defer to his formidable wife.

However, Mary feels that her father has always been less hostile than her mother to the idea of her relationship with Tommy, the likeable, dependable son of his friend and workmate from the shipyard, George Nelson. *There's hope there, surely?*

A shudder suddenly runs through Mary. *Thank God Billy wasn't in the house. He would have stood by me, against her. Billy would always stand by me, no matter what.* Nobody would ever dare so much as lift a finger to any of the McNally sisters in Billy's presence. *Nobody.*

So, what now?

I don't know.

Where do I go?

I don't know.

Will I tell Tommy?

No!

No, I can't tell Tommy! Not anything! Not yet. Not until he's here with me, by my side. It wouldn't be fair. He has enough to think about over there, it's enough for him just to concentrate on... staying alive. God help me, I can't distract him from that, I can't take the chance. Oh Tommy, come back soon to me my love and take me away! Please, just take me away!

Her mother is still crying in her room as Mary leaves the house, carrying a small suitcase packed with a few changes of clothes and some other necessities. She walks briskly down Bluebell Avenue, her tearful eyes downcast. The street is mercifully deserted, save for two little girls playing outside on the pavement, too engrossed in fixing their dollies' hair to even notice Mary as she passes by. She turns right at the end of Bluebell Avenue and walks on despondently, aimlessly down the street, past Beattie's shop, towards town.

Mary's melancholy, solitary trudge through the bustling streets of Belfast eventually ends at the top of Cavehill. Exhausted and sore, Mary slowly removes her shoes and stockings with a grimace, and stands looking down over the city, the feeling of the cool grass against her blistered feet a blissful relief. *Oh Tommy, I'm so afraid. I have never felt so alone. How I wish you were here again with me now, my love.* Mary closes her eyes for a moment. Suddenly, from nowhere, the notion of simply walking over the edge pops into her mind unbidden. Her eyes fly wide open in alarm at the unwanted, alien thought. *Never!*

What would her death accomplish, in any case, save only to cause but further anguish to those she loved? She gazes down once more over the silent city. *No.* The world and its people would go on regardless - go on loving each other, hating each other, living, dying, making love, making war, oblivious to the fate of an unmarried nineteen-year-old girl and her unborn child.

She puts her hand protectively on her belly. *No. Life must go on. WE must go on, dear baby. I don't know how yet, but it's going to be alright. I'll make it alright for you. For Tommy. For me. For us all.*

With a tired sigh, Mary sits on the grass and rummages through her little suitcase, eventually retrieving her letter-paper and pencil. She chews the top of the pencil for a moment, resisting the urge to just let *everything* simply gush out onto the page, and begins to write a letter to Tommy.

Night is beginning to fall over Belfast when Mary eventually limps her way back up Bluebell Avenue. Utterly spent, she shambles up to the front door of the house, letting her suitcase fall to the ground beside her. *Oh God, Please.* She gives two weary knocks on the door and waits, her shattered mind filled with hope and dread in equal measure at what may come.

After what seems like an eternity, the door is opened by a kindly-looking middle-aged woman who takes one look at the swollen, tear-streaked face of the exhausted girl teetering in front of her, and lets out a small cry of alarm, her hand covering her mouth in shock. 'Good *Lord!* Whatever's the matter, Mary dear?'

Mary, her last reserves of strength gone, collapses into the strong but gentle arms of Iris Nelson.

CHAPTER SEVEN

Somme, 30ᵗʰ June, 1916

The smell of the War welcomes them back to the British front-line trench, which zig-zags its way through the shattered, charred remains of Thiepval Wood. The pungent ammoniac stink of explosives all but drowns out the evil *mélange* of ordure, urine, and decaying flesh.

It is the seventh day of the heaviest artillery bombardment the world has ever seen - a continuous, terrifying, insane, rolling thunder of nearly fifteen hundred field pieces of all calibres firing in concert. The very air overhead is alive with screaming metal as salvo after salvo of artillery shells roars over to pulverise the German positions beyond.

The men of the Ulster Division throng the trench. Those on watch man the fire-steps, grim-faced. Others busy themselves cleaning, checking, and re-checking the actions of their Lee-Enfields and Lewis guns. Those fortunate enough to be off-duty sit smoking, drinking tea, bantering, and scratching at their lice.

Tommy Nelson sits alone with his thoughts, grimacing as he sips a mugful of trench tea that sports the unmistakable tang of petrol. He looks up unenthusiastically as Davey, whose lips are still slightly swollen from his misadventure in the *estaminet*, saunters cheerfully down the trench towards him, his Brodie helmet cocked jauntily on his head.

' 'Bout ye, Tommy?'

' 'Bout ye, Davey', Tommy states as flatly and discouragingly as he can manage without resorting to overt offence.

Davey, undeterred, nods to Tommy's cup. 'Is the tae not agreein' with ye Tommy, or what?'

'Not at all. I just fockin' love the taste o' petrol, so I do – ya wee lemon, ye!'

Davey juts out his chin boldly, flashing a tight grin that doesn't quite reach his eyes. 'Where's yer Taig mucker McNally today then, Tommy? Takin' it easy after knockin' the shite out o' that big Dublin heavy bag the other night?'

Tommy sighs. *Here we go. Stay calm, Nelson. Every time, I swear I'll not let the hateful little shite wind me up but I just can't help meself.* 'What's yer problem Davey? I'm startin' to get a wee bit tired of yer shite, so I am.'

'Ye know *exactly* what my problem is, Tommy. It's yer little Fenian friend, McNally, so it is.'

Tommy rises angrily, his mug falling to floor of the trench, spilling the dregs of the unsavoury brew onto the duckboards. 'Billy McNally's no *Fenian*, Patterson! He's over here wearin' khaki just like the rest of us. Some sort o' quare fockin' Fenian *that* is!'

Davey sneers. 'He's a Taig, isn't he? It's the same fockin' thing to *me!* I dunno why ye're so chummy with him, so I don't. I mean, whoever heard of a fockin' Taig called Billy, anyways?'

'Why d'ye *hate* him so much, Patterson? Ye don't even know the man.'

'I've never known a good Taig yet, so I haven't.'

'Ye've never known one in yer *life* at all, ye mean.'

Davey shrugs. 'Aye, well, I don't ever care to either, Nelson. I don't trust *him*, or *any* of 'em!' He prods himself emphatically in the chest with his index finger. '*I* know why *I'm* here, Tommy! *I'm loyal. I'm* fightin' for God and Ulster. King and Empire. No Home Rule! No *Rome Rule!* What the hell's *he* doin' here?!

67

'He's here fightin' the Hun, same as you and me, isn't he, Sherlock?'

Davey replies through clenched teeth. 'Yer a funny mawn, Nelson, so ye are. I'll tell ye, McNally's only here cos his Parish Priest told him to go and save poor little Catholic Belgium. Loyal to a Roman dictator! Not to the Crown, *nor* to Ulster, I'm tellin' ye!'

'Ach, yer talkin' through yer hole so ye are, Patterson! Look, aren't we all in the shite here together now, fightin' the same fight?' Tommy smirks at Davey provocatively. 'Oh, and by the way, in case ye hadn't noticed, Patterson, ya lemon, we're not *in* Belgium! The Somme's in poor Catholic France, so it is! Yer a confused, angry wee mawn, so ye are!'

Davey points his finger aggressively at Tommy. 'Don't be fockin' pullin' the piss outta *me*, Nelson! If *I'm* confused then I'm not the *only* one who is 'round here, that's fer sure! What about *ye*, smart mawn? I know where *my* loyalty lies, but what about *ye*? Ye'd take the side of a Taig against one of yer own, would ye?'

Tommy takes an angry, ominous step closer to Davey. *'One of my own? Loyalty? I'm Ulster to my bones, ya wee shite, ya!* Now listen to me, Patterson! I *grew up* with Billy McNally, so I did. We've been boxin' together since we're five years old! I've never yet judged the measure of a man by where he chooses to say his prayers of a Sunday mornin' and, to be honest, I don't give a shite! We're *all* God's children, Patterson, ye know.' Tommy nods his head curtly up towards the German lines, not three hundred yards distant. 'Even *those* buggers up there! I'm tellin' ye now that I'd trust Billy McNally with my *life*, so I would. *That's* loyalty too for ye, Patterson! He's like a brother to me and I'll not see him blackguarded by you or anyone! So watch yer mouth, Davey boy. I *mean* that. Are ye hearin' me? Cos I'm warnin' ye for the last time, now!'

Davey squares up to Tommy, his finger jabbing closer to Tommy's chest, his face contorted by anger and bitterness. 'Ye don't scare *me*, Mr. big-shite boxer! Ye, *OR* yer Taig-boy!'

Davey never sees the punch coming, Tommy's lightning straight right landing squarely on the young man's jaw, knocking him to the ground before he even realises he has been hit. Tommy, his blood up, stands triumphantly over him. 'Now go home tae yer Mammy, ya wee shite, ya!'

'*What* the bloody hell is goin' on here, lads?' The usually jovial tone of Serjeant Andy McNair is now cold and replete with authority. 'Rifleman Patterson! On yer feet! *Now!*'

Davey gets slowly and sullenly to his feet, rubbing his jaw. Andy regards him sternly. 'Is there somethin' ye want to get off yer chest, boy?'

Davey glares dourly at Tommy as he replies. 'No, Sarn't! Slipped in the bloody mud, so I did. Rifleman Nelson here was just about to help me up.'

Andy turns to Tommy. 'Is that the truth of it, Rifleman Nelson?'

Tommy nods, returning Davey's stare. 'Aye, Sarn't McNair.'

Andy's joviality makes a brief return. 'Ach, Good lads! Grand, so. Well, that's that, then.' He treats Davey to a withering glare, his voice cold again. 'It fockin' *better* be! Now, Private Patterson, I hear we've received some post back at Battalion Headquarters, so we have. Be so good as tae go and fetch it for me, would ye?'

Davey looks sullenly from Tommy to Andy. He acknowledges Andy's order with a grudging 'Aye, Sarn't', then saunters off back along the trench.

Andy turns to Tommy, grinning. 'Well, he can be a gubby wee shite, so he can, but at least he's no rat, I'll give him that. What was the story there, Tommy? A friendly wee discussion about yer mucker McNally, I take it?'

Tommy sighs. 'Aye, you could say that, Sarn't. Unfortunately, we had a slight difference of opinion, though. Billy McNally's a good man, ye know, Sarn't – and Patterson has had that lampin' comin' for a long time now, so he has.'

Andy nods in agreement. 'Ach, I don't doubt ye. Young McNally can certainly fockin' fight, so he can. God knows we need fighters! Look, I'll be honest, Nelson, I'm as loyal an Ulsterman as any, but as long as a man is a good soldier, is willin' to fight, and can fockin' follow orders, that's all that counts in my book. Some lads, like Davey, can't see that's really *all* that matters, but mark my words, he'll change his tune when the shite starts to fly around here tomorrow. I learnt that the *hard* way, fightin' the Boers, so I did. And bloody lucky I was to survive the lesson, I can tell ye! Nearly did for me twice, so they did, the buggers! Now yer mawn Smuts is on *our* side, fightin' against the Hun!'

Andy shakes his head in bemusement. 'It's a funny oul' world I'm tellin' ye! Look lad, Davey's angry cos he lost his only brother a few months ago in the Dublin rebellion. He's never told anyone. I only know cos I was there with his brother in the Third Reserve Battalion when he was killed. Norman Patterson was a good lad. A rebel sniper took him with a headshot in Camden Street, so he did, the wee bastard.'

Andy spits on the ground in disgust. 'Norman never stood a chance. He was killed instantly, so he was, the poor lad. The Army were goin' to bury him down there in Dublin in the Military Cemetery in Grangegorman, so they were, but the family would have none of it. The Pattersons wanted to bring poor Norman home to Belfast, cos they couldn't bear the thought of their eldest boy lyin' in the clay down there in Dublin, so they couldn't.'

Andy lowers his voice conspiratorially. 'He's a Reverend, ye know, is Mr. Patterson. Church of Ireland... I'm Presbyterian meself, but not a very good one, I'd be the first to admit!' As if to reinforce the point, Andy produces a small hip flask and offers it to Tommy, who gratefully takes a good, long swig before handing the flask back to Andy.

'But Sarn't, how come Davey's never said anythin'? About his brother, I mean?'

'*Ahhh!*' Andy savours the fiery whiskey, wetting his whistle thoroughly before continuing. 'I'm not sure, lad. I think he's afraid to, and ye can call me Andy by the way, when we're by ourselves.'

72

'Afraid to? I'm not sure I follow ye... Andy.'

'Well, in a word – *hate*, lad. Hate's a precious thing to some people, ye know. So, they guard it carefully, cos it keeps them goin'. Sometimes, ye see, it's the *only* thing that keeps them goin'. Davey Patterson is just a scared wee boy, really. He's full o' hate over the death of his brother, so he is, and yer mucker McNally just happens to be a handy wee target for him. But that hate is keeping Davey goin', so it is, and he's afraid o' spakin' o' Norman in case it might slip away on him, and then he'd be left with... Well, nothin', I suppose.'

Tommy regards Andy gravely. 'Shite, I'd better tell Billy, or I'm afraid he'll kill Davey before we even get the chance to go over the top tomorrow! Sher, I'm just after layin' Davey out meself! I told him that he was a confused, angry wee man, so I did, and he didn't take too kindly to it.'

Andy gives his moustache another pensive twiddle. 'Aye, he's all that, right enough, and more! Ach, don't be worryin' yerself about it, laddie. At half past seven tomorrow mornin' when the Ruperts blow their whistles, it won't matter much anymore. Look, in the meantime, tell yer mucker to pay no heed to what young Patterson says. Like I said, he's only a scared wee boy behind the hard mawn act, so he is. Ye'll see, it'll be the *Hun* that'll catch hell from him tomorrow!'

Tommy frowns broodingly. 'Ye've been to war before, Andy. Tell us the truth, now... What's it going to be like tomorrow, really?'

Andy looks hard at Tommy for a moment, then sighs. 'Well, the Red Tabs would have us believe that after a continuous, week-long bombardment, the German wire will be cut, and there'll be nothin' left alive up there come tomorrow mornin'. It'll literally be a walk-over for us.'

Tommy looks searchingly at the veteran Serjeant as a salvo of eighteen-pounder shells roars overhead, exploding in No-Mans-Land in a thunderous series of blasts. 'And what do *you* think, Andy?'

Andy pauses for moment to consider his reply. He nods in the direction of the blasts from the recent salvo. 'Well, for one thing, our artillery has been firin' mostly shrapnel shells, instead of high explosive, for the past week. That's not going to do much as regards cuttin' the wire, for a start, lad. Bad news, that is.'

He tugs distractedly again at his moustache. 'The other thing is, those buggers up there are well dug in, so they are. They'll have concrete bunkers up there dug in maybe thirty, forty feet deep, so they will. That's German industry and organisation for ye, boy! Ye can fire any fockin' thing ye like up at those

74

bunkers and it's not goin' to do much except piss off whoever's inside. Fair enough, they've probably been without supplies for the best part of a week cos of our bombardment, so they'll be hungry, thirsty, and *well* pissed-off. But they'll be *alive*. And when our barrage stops and the whistles blow, they'll be waitin' for us, so they will.' Andy licks his lips uneasily. 'That's what *I* think, lad.'

Horror descends over Tommy like a malevolent black curtain. '*Jesus Christ, Andy...*'

Andy gives a short, bitter laugh. 'Aye, lad. I'm startin' to think more and more about *Him* meself the closer tomorrow mornin' gets!'

Andy forces a smile in an effort to banish the gloom, and pats Tommy on the shoulder reassuringly. 'Look, lad, if it's one thing an Ulsterman knows how to do, it's box, and box *clever*, at that. Our own Brass Hats will have somethin' up their sleeves for tomorrow mornin'. They'll have some surprise in store for the Hun, so they will. I'm *sure* of it!'

Tommy still looks appalled. 'I certainly fockin' hope so, Andy, or there'll be a lot o' mammies back in Ulster gettin' telegrams come next week, so there will!'

The veteran Serjeant tries his best to remain upbeat. 'Well, one thing ye can count on, Tommy, is that we'll give it a bloody good go, and that's fer sure! So, chin up, now! Ach, you wait and see, boy! We'll make the shite fly out of the Hun tomorrow! We'll be goin' in with the bayonet, ye know! We'll see *then* how oul' Fritz fancies a good big dose o' cold Sheffield steel! Sher, I know it'll be hard goin' right enough, but we're *Ulstermen*, Tommy! No Surrender, eh?

Tommy, looking subdued, regards Andy doubtfully. 'Aye. No Surrender...'

Andy strokes his moustache again thoughtfully and decides to change the subject. 'Ahem, Tommy, if ye don't mind me askin', how come youse two are so chummy? Yerself and McNally, I mean? It's a bit... unusual, to be honest about it, ye know.'

'Me and Billy grew up next door to each other in Bluebell Avenue, so we did. We started boxin' together when we were weans. We were always gettin' into all sorts o' shite together.'

Tommy smiles at the memory. 'Always fightin', so we were, the pair of us! If we weren't fightin' each other we'd be fightin' the Murphys from Gertrude Street, or the Bells from Fraser Street! Sometimes, only the *very odd time* now, mind, we'd

76

even take it handy, so we would, and watch the Murphys and the Bells lamp *each other!'*

Andy chuckles as Tommy continues enthusiastically. 'We started in the shipyard together, ye know. We'd walk there in the mornin' with our Das. After work, we'd walk back with them in the evenin', home just in time for tae, the men o' the house, proud as punch, like the fockin' Kings o' East Belfast!'

Tommy lowers his voice, as if about to impart a marvellous secret. 'Billy has a wee sister called Mary. Did ye see her at the parade back in Belfast, when we were on home leave? I swear to God, Andy, she's the bonniest lass Belfast City ever saw, so she is! We've been coortin' since I was seventeen, and she was fourteen. We got engaged just before we shipped back to Seaford!'

Andy gives a little whistle of surprise. 'Oh, I remember *her* alright! My *word*, lad! *Engaged!* To a Taig girl? You're a mad wee focker, Nelson, so ye are, d'ye know that?!'

Tommy grins somewhat bashfully. 'Aye, maybe so! But I did it the oul' fashioned way, Andy, so I did! I was out for a dander in town one Saturday afternoon, when I passed by Lendrum's window. Ye know, the jewellers on Royal Avenue? Well, I knew I wanted the ring *straight away* when I saw it! A lovely wee solitaire, so it was, just *perfect* for my Mary! So, I

77

started savin' up the docket week after week from the shipyard, then the Army, for Lord knows how long! I never said a word about it to Mary, nor anyone else, so I didn't! Then, the other day, nervous as shite, I went into Lendrum's and bought it. It nearly fockin' burnt a hole in me britches pocket before I managed to pluck up the courage to ask her!'

The two men look at each other and burst out laughing. Tommy lowers his voice again to a conspiratorial whisper. *'I had it all planned, ye know.* It was Sunday 23rd April. After she'd been to Mass and I'd been to Service, we met up and snuck off for a wee picnic up Cavehill, so we did. After the picnic, we stood at the top o' the hill and looked down over Belfast, laid out before us at our feet, like we were the King and Queen o' the city! Then I says to her, "What's that on yer toe, love?" I bent down on one knee fast, whipped the wee box out o' me pocket, and put it on the toe of her shoe! She bent down and picked up the box, her wee hands shakin'. Then I asked her to marry me. *Yes!* She said *YES*, Andy, and I was the happiest man in the whole of Ulster!'

Andy grins, rolling his eyes in jest at Tommy. 'I'd never've figured ye for such a romantic eejit Tommy, but congratulations, mate! You're a lucky wee shite so ye are! How are ye going to manage it though? Gettin' married, I mean?'

Tommy pauses, suddenly looking despondent once more. 'Ach, I don't know Andy. At the moment, I'm findin' it hard tae think any further ahead than tomorrow mornin', so I am. All I know is that we'll *find* a way to make it happen! Sometime after all this shite is over, please God. Then we're off tae America or Canada, so we are.'

'What'll yer Ma and Da say, Tommy? Did ye tell them?', Andy asks gently.

Tommy shakes his head. 'Not yet. They've known the McNally's all their lives, so they have, but I'll be honest with ye - I'm not sure how they'll take it - especially me Da. But look, I'm a grown mawn, Andy. I love me Ma and Da but it's *my* life and I'll live it as I please, *with* whoever I please. But they're good people, and even if they don't approve at first, I know they'll come around in time. Ma's always been very fond of Mary, so she has. There's hope there.'

For a brief moment, Andy McNair looks as if he is very far away. 'Aye... *Hope*', he mumbles vaguely.

'Andy? Are ye alright?'

'Oh aye, Tommy. Sorry, lad - I was miles away there for a minute, so I was... Anyway, what about *her* Ma and Da?'

'Mary's not told *them* yet, either. I think her Da will be okay about it all, but I'm not so sure about her Ma. She was never gone on the notion of Mary and I seein' each other. Not like *that*, anyway - romantically and all - I mean. Anyway, we decided to hang on and tell them *all* together, so we did.'

Tommy smiles bitterly. 'So, now the ring's burnin' a hole in *Mary's* pocket, so tae spake - she's wearin' it on a chain actually - until I get back. Then we'll tell 'em all, and tae hell with the begrudgers!'

'Good fer *ye*, mate! Does Billy know ye're engaged?'

'Aye, he knows alright. He's goin' to be my Best Man, o' course!' Tommy regards Andy curiously. 'How about you, mate? Are ye married? Have ye anyone waitin' fer ye at home?'

Andy lets out a long, melancholy sigh. 'I *was* married, mate. She died a long time ago, havin' our babby, so she did. But there isn't a day goes by that I don't think of my Annie, or Rory, our poor wee babby, so there isn't.'

Tommy bows his head sadly. 'I'm so sorry, mate. I truly am.'

Andy smiles a sorrowful smile. 'Ach, yer grand, laddie. It was a long time ago, like I said. Now, it's just me and me oul' Ma. She's gettin' on a bit now, o' course, but she's doin' grand, all the same. She's keepin' the home fires burnin' back in Lendrick Street, so she is, til her boy comes home. To be honest with ye, Tommy, I often wonder would I be here talkin' to ye at all if things had worked out differently. After Annie and wee Rory died, I wasn't doin' too well fer a while, so I decided to leave Belfast and try me luck in Canada, so I did. Sher if they'd lived, maybe we'd all have upped sticks and gone and made a new go of it over there, so we would. Just like ye and Mary are plannin' to do. It's a pity, though, that now I'll never know.'

Andy swallows hard and swipes his hand slowly across his mouth, composing himself. 'Anyways, I was over there drinkin' hard, driftin' from town to town, and from shite job to shite job, but eventually Ulster called me home, lad, so she did. In between the jigs and the reels, I decided to re-enlist in the Royal Irish Rifles. Soldierin' is the only life I've ever known, really, lad - it's certainly the only bloody thing I've ever been good at! Well, they were lookin' for men with experience to help train the new lads comin' in, so they were. That's how I found meself in the Third Reserve Battalion in Dublin this Easter, in the middle of a fockin' rebellion!' Andy guffaws. 'Now, I find meself here on the Somme, getting ready for the biggest fockin' battle in history! Never a dull moment for Mrs. McNair's wee boy, eh Tommy?'

Tommy grins, nodding his agreement. 'That's for sure, mate.' Pausing, he looks down pensively, his grin faltering. 'The whole bloody world is tearin' its own arse asunder, so it is. Now Ulster has called her sons, and we'll not let her down! But look, I'll be straight with ye, Andy - fightin' for God and Ulster, and fightin' for King and Empire, they're all grand things to be fightin' for, so they are, but I'm fightin' for those I hold dear, most of all. Billy and me have been lookin' out for each other since we were weans, ye know. I'm fightin' to bring that lad back home to Belfast, safe and sound, so I am, and for my Mary. It's *her* I'm fightin' for most of all, Andy. I don't care if the entire German Army is standin' in my way, I'll fockin' *wade* through their *blood* if I have to, to get back to her!'

Andy nods gravely. 'Ach, I understand, Tommy. Yer a good man, so ye are. Sher, when all's said and done, we can only do our best, lad, any of us! For our country, for our families, and for each other. The rest is in God's hands. *Quis Separabit,* mate. Who shall divide us?'

As Tommy and Andy solemnly shake hands, a German shell explodes just beyond the parapet of the trench, forcing the two men to dive for cover. They rise slowly from the duckboards, leaning on each other and grinning helplessly at the simple marvel of mutual survival. As muck continues to rain down on them from the explosion, Davey Patterson zigzags his way back down the trench towards them, carrying a bag of mail.

' 'Bout ye lads?' Billy McNally, his face still bearing the scars of the *Battle of the Estaminet,* returns from a working party at the opposite end of the trench. He spots Davey, and the two men regard each other warily for a moment in hostile silence.

' 'Bout ye, mate!' Tommy motions for his friend to sit down beside him.

'Give out the letters like a good lad, will ye?' Andy orders Davey. 'Time is pushin' and shovin' on, so it is.'

'Aye, Sarn't.' Davey opens the mail bag and sullenly begins to hand out their precious letters from home. Billy takes his letter in silence from Davey, the two men glaring malevolently at each other. Just as the men begin to open their letters, the tall, hawkish figure of Captain McAllister comes striding down the trench.

'TEN-*SHUN!*'

At Andy's command, the men bolt up to attention and salute Captain McAllister, which he returns with a casual flick of his hand.

'Righto - stand easy, lads. I just want a quick word with ye.' McAllister regards Billy sternly. 'First off, I heard ye bate the shite out of the Dublin Fusiliers' champion the other night, McNally!'

'Wasn't me, Sir!' The automatic, unerring, universal response of enlisted men everywhere. Davey looks away disgustedly as the other soldiers burst into laughter.

McAllister gives a canny smile. 'Bullshite, McNally! Ye can't keep somethin' like that a secret for long around here, so ye can't! Half the Division's talkin about it, fer God's sake! Ach, don't be worryin' yerself about it, lad. Ye'll get no trouble from me for knockin' the stuffin' out of a Royal Dublin Fusilier! That's braggin' rights over those Dublin shites for a wee while anyway, eh, Sarn't McNair?'

'Absolutely, Sir!'

'Just make it official the next time, lads, eh? Come to me and I'll organise it for ye. Sher it'd be a grand night out for the whole battalion, so it would. Nothin' like a good oul' challenge match to boost morale, especially if it's the Southern boys on the end of a hidin'! Ach, sher none o' them are any match for a true blue Ulsterman, eh McNally?'

Billy clears his throat noisily. 'Well, no match for a Royal Irish Rifleman anyway, Sir.'

Colours floods McAllister's face. 'Ahem. Of course, McNally, of course. Well, ye've done the Regiment *and* the Division proud, lad, so ye have. Well done!'

'Thank ye, Sir!'

'Look, spakin' o' challenges, men, I want tae spake to ye about the attack tomorrow mornin'.' McAllister sighs, removes his Brodie helmet and scratches his head for a moment. 'Look, I'll give it to ye straight lads.' He replaces his helmet. 'Those of ye who aren't blind and deaf will know that for the past week now, our artillery has been poundin' the shite out of the German positions all along the Somme sector. The objective of this, of course, is to obliterate the enemy's wire obstructions, destroy his defensive positions, and generally kill as many enemy soldiers as possible! Now I'm sure ye've all heard that when the attack begins tomorrow mornin', all we'll have to do is climb out of this trench and toddle up to those German lines like we're goin' for a wee dander of a Saturday mornin'!'

The men break into nervous, somewhat uneasy laughter. Another German shell lands just beyond the parapet, the explosion showering the trench with muck, stones, and splinters. As the men flinch and duck for cover, Captain

McAllister makes an emphatic, truly officer-like show of remaining completely calm and unaffected - a simple adjustment of his helmet, which has been knocked slightly awry by a falling clod of earth - being his sole acknowledgement of the explosive interruption.

McAllister continues as if the explosion had never happened, casting a reproving eye in the direction of the Schwaben Redoubt, as if challenging the Germans to try it again, if they dared. 'Ye may also have heard that we will be able to advance in such a fashion because no enemy soldier could *possibly* be left alive up there after such a bombardment, and if any *do* remain alive, then they will be completely incapacitated due to shock and/or injury! Aye! And maybe ye've all figured out by now that this notion is a pile of *horseshite*, so it is!'

Captain McAllister grins as he precipitates a heartier laugh from the men, realising that they are now beginning to respond to his easy authority. 'Now, as soon as our barrage ceases, the enemy will be expectin' us to go over the top and stroll up yonder wee hill, givin' him plenty of time to come up out of his bunkers and man his machine guns. Well, we're goin' to steal a march on these buggers, lads, so we are!'

'Beggin' yer pardon, Captain McAllister', Andy pipes up, 'But how d'ye mean, Sir?'

McAllister turns to Andy self-assuredly. 'Well, Serjeant, I'll tell ye exactly how! At oh-seven-ten hours tomorrow, while our barrage is still blastin' the shite out of the Hun positions, we're goin' down the Russian Saps into No Man's Land and advancin' to within one hundred and fifty yards of the German front line. We will remain in position there until oh-seven-thirty hours. That's Zero Hour, lads, at which time the general attack will commence all along the line. We'll have a head start, so tae spake, lads. We'll advance at the double and we'll be on top of those buggers before they know what's hit 'em! Lieutenant Colonel Crozier and Lieutenant Colonel Bernard will be leadin' the attack personally, so they will! Remember, it's the First of July tomorrow lads. Ye'll do the Regiment, the Division, *and* Ulster proud, of that I've no doubt!'

'*YES, SIR!*' the men cry enthusiastically, as one. Captain McAllister nods in satisfaction. 'That's grand so, lads, that'll be all for the moment. Carry on! Oh, and make sure and get yer letters sorted soon now, too!' McAllister flicks out a salute, which is smartly returned by the men, and then he is gone.

There is a brief lull in the artillery barrage. Tommy looks around at the faces of the other men. 'Well lads, what d'ye make of all that?'

'I told ye our Brass Hats would come up with some manner of trickery, so I did, Tommy!' Andy replies excitedly, nervously twiddling one side of his moustache, then the other. 'Sounds grand, doesn't it? It's not perfect, I know, but sher what plan ever is?'

Andy pauses, chewing his lip pensively. 'The only thing is, we're dependin' on the lads in the Twenty-Ninth and Thirty-Second Divisions, on either side of us, to take their objectives. Otherwise, our arses'll be hangin' out in the wind, so they will. The Hun will be able to pour fire into us from the flanks, and – '

'The goin' could get rough?', Billy ventures.

Andy regards Billy gravely. 'Aye, lad. You *could* say that, I suppose. It could be rough goin' alright, but – '

A distant, lone, youthful voice echoes down from the German front line. 'Hey, Paddy! The English are killing your women and children on the streets of Dublin!'

At the mention of Dublin, Davey Patterson's face contorts, and he gasps involuntarily, as if punched in the stomach. He bounds up onto the firestep, much to Andy's alarm. *'Careful, Davey!'*

Ignoring the Serjeant, Davey cups his hands over his mouth and roars up towards the German positions. 'We're *Ulstermen*, ye stupid wee bastard, ye!'

Billy regards Davey forlornly as the rest of the men give a tremendous, lusty Ulster cheer and begin to sing -

God save our gracious King!

Long live our noble King!

God save our King!

Send him victorious!

Happy and glorious!

Long to reign over us! -

Their song is interrupted by the *THOCK* of a German bullet smacking into a sandbag on the parapet, making Davey and a roving, corpse-fattened trench rat dive for cover. The report from the sniper's rifle follows just after, drifting lazily down from the Schwaben Redoubt. The loathsome rodent scuttles off down the trench, pausing to look back in disgust at Davey, who rises from the duckboards self-consciously, shakily raising his hand to his head as if to make sure it is still there.

'Shite, that was a close one! I felt the fockin' wind from that one, so I did! Look at the size o' the fockin' hole in that sandbag! The bastards are firin' dum-dums, so they are!'

Andy guffaws helplessly. 'Well, they can't be much good if they're not able tae hit *yer* fockin' big head, Davey, ya lemon! It must be our singin' voices, lads! Sher, I didn't think we were *that* bad!' He cups his hands over his mouth and shouts up towards the German lines. 'Ye can't shoot for shite, Fritz! Ye'll have tae do better than *that*, so ye will, or yer all focked, the lot o' ye!'

The same youthful German voice echoes down to the Ulstermen. 'Fuck *you*, Tommy!'

Andy winks at the other men. 'Yer *mother*, Fritz!'

Andy's swift comeback prompts wild hooting from the Ulstermen. The young German, apparently bested, remains silent.

Tommy claps Andy on the back. '*That* shut the bastards up, so it did, Sarn't! Round one to the Ulstermen, lads!'

Andy's voice eventually cuts through the raucous cheering that erupts from the men. 'Right lads! Enough o' the shite! Ye heard what the Captain said! Time tae get yer letters sorted, now! Time's pushin' and shovin' on, ye know, so let's get to it!'

As wave after incessant wave of shellfire continues again to thunder over them, the men settle down as best they can. As the evening wears on, they withdraw to whatever privacy they can manage, reading and writing their letters with an intensity born of the sobering realisation that it may be for the last time.

CHAPTER EIGHT

Somme, 30th June, 1916

Mrs. Hilda McNair,

72 Lendrick Street,

Belfast.

Monday, 29th May, 1916

Serjeant Andrew McNair,

B Coy., - Battalion,

Royal Irish Rifles.

My Dearest Andy,

I hope this letter finds you well. I do hope that you are behaving yourself now, and that you are not being too hard on those poor boys over there! Sure they are only weans, most of them. I am in good health son, so promise me now that you won't be doing any worrying on my account.

Mrs. Davis next door is very good to me. She comes in once a week and does a bit of washing and cleaning for me. The woman is an absolute angel, and I don't know what I'd do without her! She has three boys of her own at the front, as you know, so she has her own worries, of course. Sometimes she sits up with me at night and we drink tae til the wee hours. She talks about her Jonny, and Stuart, and Mark, and tells me all their news, and I talk about you, my brave Andy. How those three boys used to look up to ye when they were weans! Your Da would be so proud of you, Son, if he were still alive. Please look after yourself Andy, as you are all that I have left now, my dear son.

My heart aches when I see how much other families here have sacrificed in this awful war. I think my heart really would break if anything were to happen to you, Andy. I know the young lads over there probably look up to you, but please don't do anything foolish, or try and be a hero, my son. Please just do your duty, and then come home safe to your old Ma. I'll make you the biggest Ulster Fry that you ever saw in your life!

Please write soon Andy, as I treasure each and every letter! Goodbye for now son, and mind yourself.

Love,

Ma.

93

P.S. Don't forget to say your prayers!

P.P.S. The only real trouble I have here is trying to get to sleep at night, what with that ratten wee tramp Lottie Spencer's terrier barking all night across the street, the dirty wee shite!

    God Bless,

        Ma.

The Reverend S. W. Patterson Esq.,

The Rectory,

Glengarry Street,

Belfast.

Sunday, 28th May, 1916

Rifleman David Patterson,

B Coy., - Battalion,

Royal Irish Rifles.

My Dearest David,

We haven't had any news from you for some time now, so I thought I might take this opportunity write to you, my dear son. The recent loss of your brother Norman in such tragic and appalling circumstances has, of course, been a terrible blow to our whole family, but I fear, my dear son, that you have been the one most deeply and sadly affected by his death.

I have the utmost faith, David, that Norman is in Paradise, seated at the right hand of the Lord. It is we who are left behind who must carry the burden of grief and sorrow. But we must also continue to live, my son. Your brother, fine Christian man that he was, would not wish it any other way for us, and especially, my dearest David, for you.

We must try to let go of hate and bitterness my son, for they serve no ultimate purpose except to damage ourselves and those we love. We are living in dark and turbulent times, David. Unfortunately, it has fallen upon a generation of brave young men like yourself and your brother to restore peace and order to a world sundered by war and violence. May the Good Lord bless and keep you all over there, my son. May He maketh His Face to shine upon your endeavours, and keep you all steadfast in your faith.

Faith! Ah, such sacrifice! Sometimes the magnitude of it threatens to overwhelm me! My dearest David, in the darkest moments of whatever trials may come, remember to seek the peace and comfort of the Lord in the words of the Twenty-Third Psalm, as I so often do:

> *The LORD is my Shepherd; I shall not want.*

> *He maketh me to lie down in green pastures: He leadeth me beside the still waters.*

> *He restoreth my soul: He leadeth me in the paths of righteousness for His name's sake.*

> *Yea, though I walk through the valley of the shadow of death, I will fear no evil: for Thou art with me; Thy rod and Thy staff they comfort me.*

Thou preparest a table before me in the presence of mine enemies: Thou anointest my head with oil; my cup runneth over.

Surely goodness and mercy shall follow me all the days of my life: and I will dwell in the house of the LORD *forever.*

Words cannot express how proud I am of you, my son. Please write soon, if and when you get the chance. It would mean so much to your mother, your sister, and I. We love you and pray constantly for your safe return, my dear David. May the good Lord preserve you in your times of need, and guide you home safely. His Will be done.

I remain,

Your loving father.

Friday, 26th May, 1916

Rifleman William McNally,

B Coy., - Battalion,

Royal Irish Rifles.

Dear Billy,

I hope all is well with you son, wherever you are in France, and that the conditions are not too bad for you there. Remember to eat up all your grub now, and to get your head down whenever you get the chance!

All is grand here, son. Siobhán and Deirdre send their love, and have promised me they will write to you soon. Your Ma sends her love too. She has a bit of a cold on her, so she is just having a wee lie down at the moment. She worries so much, does my Brigid! She just needs a wee rest, I think, and she'll be as right as rain again in a day or two. I think she's worn out with all the prayers she has been saying for you lately! Anyway, I *thought that I'd take advantage of the peace and quiet to drop you a few lines!*

Mary sends her love, and no doubt she will be writing to you herself soon. She said to tell you that Annie Frost was asking for you as well, you know. Annie is a nice wee girl, Billy, and you might consider sending her a letter sometime son, if you get the chance.

Things are pretty much the same in the shipyard son, with not as much tension as usual. Most of the Prods and the Taigs have other things on their minds now than killing each other - for the moment, anyway.

Jocky Ervine said to send his regards to you and young Tommy. We had some bad news there recently, son. Remember your man Jimmy Kerr, the riveter? Well, he fell about sixty feet off a scaffold there last week and was killed, the poor bugger. They say he was full of gargle, the eejit. It'll be hard times ahead now for his missus and the weans, though. We had a whip-round at work to get a few quid together for her, the poor woman, so she could at least bury him decent.

They're starting to get ready for the Twelfth here, but it is not like before. There are so few young men left around here now, it is all very muted and strange. There is a queer atmosphere around Belfast, these days. It's like the whole city is holding its breath waiting for something big to happen, but it's not quite sure what. It is almost like there is a bloody big storm coming or something, and I don't like it. It is giving me a queer heavy feeling in the pit of my stomach, so it is. George Nelson says he feels the same way.

Anyway, it's just not the same walking to and from the shipyard without the two of youse, you know! It's just too bloody quiet without ye!

I just want to tell you how proud we all are of you, son. Look after yourself now, and you had better look after young Tommy as well, for our Mary's sake. She doesn't say much, but I know that she is missing him something awful. Your mother isn't best pleased with the whole situation there, as you may have guessed, but I hope that in time she will come around. For my own part, I have always thought that Tommy is a fine young man, and I am glad that at least you have each other over there, son. If the Murphys and the Bells couldn't beat the two of youse together, then I know that the Germans don't have a chance!

You are constantly in our prayers, son. You, Tommy, and all the lads over there. God Bless you all and bring you all home safe and sound. Please send us a letter when you get the chance, and let us know how you are. I will write again soon, and so will your Ma.

Goodbye for now, son. All the very best,

Your loving father.

Miss Mary McNally,

Bluebell Avenue,

Belfast.

Saturday, 3rd June 1916

Rifleman Thomas Nelson,

B Coy., - Battalion,

Royal Irish Rifles.

My Darling Tommy,

Thank you so much for your last letter. You have no idea how much joy it gave me to hear from you after so long without any news! One must expect such delays in wartime, I suppose. I hope this letter finds you well, and my dear Billy also. I hope that my big brother is behaving himself over there and keeping away from those French girls!

My Darling Tommy, how can I explain how I feel? It is both a source of incredible anguish, and yet also a great comfort to me, to know that you and Billy are both serving together over there. My heart is filled with great hope as I know you are both looking out for each other and will let

101

nothing come between you. Then, in some moments, my heart fills with dread when I allow myself to ponder too much.

I pray for you both constantly, my love. I pray for the safe return of you both, and of all our men. Belfast is so quiet now these days, there is something wholly unnatural about the whole thing.

Daddy and the girls send their best, and as for Mam... Well, Mam is still just Mam, I'm afraid. We are not getting on too well lately, but... Enough about that! Everything blows over eventually my love, with time, and even every war must surely have its end sometime, my darling, must it not?

Oh Tommy, I cannot wait for THIS horrible war to end and for you to come back to me, my love - I feel but half a person living half a life without you. We WILL tell everyone of our joyous news - TOGETHER! I am no longer fearful, my dearest Tommy. The very thought of you gives me strength. Do NOT be worrying yourself, my darling. All is well here. I AM WELL! Save all your strength and all your energy for the trials which I know must surely lie ahead for you all, and please take comfort in the knowledge that you are constantly in my thoughts and in my prayers. Oh, how I miss you so much, my darling!

You will likely not believe me my love, but I am writing this letter from the very spot where you proposed to me (My Lord, how long ago it seems already!) Sometimes, when I am lonely, I come up here by myself and I look down upon dear old Belfast, and I think of you. I think of you standing here beside me, my love, and I can almost FEEL the touch of your hand in mine! Please know that I will always love you, my dearest Tommy, and know that I will always be here for you. I would wait for you until the end of time, my darling. Goodbye for now, my love, and God Bless.

Your Darling Mary.

CHAPTER NINE

Somme, 30th June / 1st July, 1916

As the light begins to dwindle, the storm of artillery continues unabated, illuminating the horizon every few seconds with a flashing brilliance. Tommy kisses Mary's letter, then holds it to his heart for a few moments. He folds it gently, puts it back into its envelope, and places it in his breast pocket. Overcome suddenly with emotion, Tommy puts his face in his trembling hands and tries to compose himself. Eventually, he lets out a long, shaky sigh and sits up. He fumbles in his tunic pocket again and takes out Mary's photograph, running his finger down her smiling image tenderly. *Oh Mary, my love...*

Tommy places the photograph gently on his knee, takes out a pen and some paper, and begins to write.

The seemingly interminable, agonising night vigil eventually begins to yield to the brightening east, and the early promise of a beautiful July morning. Billy quietly approaches Davey, who is on watch on the firestep. 'Nearly time for stand-to, eh?'

Davey whirls around in surprise, jumping down off the firestep to confront Billy. 'What the bloody hell are *ye* doin' here?!'

Billy takes a pace towards the young soldier. 'Sarn't McNair sent me. Told me to relieve ye, so he did.'

Davey responds through clenched teeth. 'This is McNair's idea of a fockin' *joke*, so it is!'

Billy takes another pace forward, his voice calm. 'Aye, maybe so. But the joke's on who, Patterson? You? Me? Or the whole bloody lot of us?'

Davey scoffs disgustedly. 'Ach, yer talkin' shite now, so y'are. What are ye *really* doin' here, McNally? Ye don't belong here - with *us* - so ye don't.'

'I don't think *any* fockin' human being actually *belongs* here, Patterson, so I don't. But what d'ye want to hear, Davey? That I joined up cos Father Lynch told us about the Hun rapin' nuns in Flanders, and that it was our duty to enlist to defend poor little Catholic Belgium? Or maybe that I joined up for the King's Shillin'? Or for Ireland, and the freedom of small nations? Tell me, Davey, what does it actually fockin' matter *why* any of us are here, *now*? All that matters now is that we *are* here. We all *volunteered* to be here, Davey, for whatever reason. Now we're all in the shite *together*, like it or not. German bullets won't care whether you're a Prod or a Taig, Davey. They'll kill us all just the same, so they will. All that's left now for us is to do our duty and hope to make it home alive, and preferably in one piece!'

Davey takes a step towards Billy, the two men standing now almost face-to-face. 'Yer mucker Nelson says he trusts ye with his life, so he does.'

'Aye. And I'd trust Tommy with *my* life, so I would. I *do* trust him with my life. Ye want to know why I'm here, Davey? Tommy Nelson *is* why I'm here. He's engaged to be married to my sister Mary. I'll bring him home safe to her, so I will, or I'll die tryin'.'

Davey's eyes widen in surprise as Billy continues, his voice softening. 'Look... I'm sorry about your brother, Patterson. Tommy told me what happened. Sarn't McNair said he was a good man.'

Davey looks confused for a moment, then his face contorts in anger. 'Aye!', he sobs bitterly. 'He *was* a good man! Norman was my *only* brother, so he was! And he was murdered by a gang of dirty Fenian, Taig *bastards!*'

With a heartrending cry of pure grief and despair, Davey turns away and covers his face with his hands, his body wracked by sobs. Billy chews his lip pensively, walks slowly over to Davey and, hesitatingly, puts his hand gently on the young man's shoulder, his voice a soft whisper.

'Let it go, mate. It's eatin' ye up, from the inside out, so it is. Ye have to let *him* go, Davey. He wouldn't want to see ye like this. He wouldn't want this for ye...'

Davey turns around to face Billy, his puffy, red face a mask of suffering and misery. 'I don't want to *die* here, McNally! Not in a shitehole like this! Oh Jesus, I'm such a coward! Norman was such a good, brave man, and I'm such a fockin' *yellow, wee coward!'*

'Davey, ye may be a lot o' things, but ye're no coward, mate. Ye're *here*, aren't ye?' Yer brother would be proud of ye, so he would, may he rest in peace. Yer *doin'* yer duty, mate. To God, and to Ulster. To King and Empire. To yer brother. To yerself and yer family. Ye'll do yer duty again when we go over the top, Davey, of that I've no doubt. We'll do it *together*, so we will. Yerself, me, Tommy, and McNair... Who shall divide us, eh?'

Billy, smiling, extends his hand slowly to Davey. Overcome with emotion, Davey extends his own trembling hand and grasps Billy's like a drowning man.

'I'm sorry, McNally. I'm so sorry.'

'Forget it, mate. No point looking back now, so there isn't.' Billy grins. 'Let's think about all the lovely times we've got to look forward to, instead.'

As the two men begin to laugh, Andy and Tommy arrive on the scene, leading the rest of 'B' Company down the trench. Andy winks at Tommy. 'Well, well! What have we here, then? It's a good job we weren't a German raiding party, lads, or ye'd both be stone dead now, so ye would! Some pair o' fockin' dickers, *ye are!*'

Davey clears his throat self-consciously. 'Sorry, Sarn't. Meself and Rifleman McNally were just discussin' tactics for the impending attack on the German positions, so we were!'

Andy gives a hearty laugh. 'Oh, *ye'll* be kept, Rifleman Patterson, so ye will! Ye're full o' shite so ye are, boy! Ye'll be gettin' yer stripes, so ye will, if ye're not careful!'

Andy continues, his demeanour now more serious. 'Look, we'll be goin' over the top soon, so we will, lads. I just want to wish ye all good luck and shake ye by the hand. It's been a pleasure, so it has!' He looks intently at each of the men. 'Now listen! When it all kicks off, move fast! Stick close to me, but remember, don't bunch up too much, either! Don't give Fritz an easy target! And when we get to the top up there, fockin' give it to 'im with whatever ye have! Bayonet, bullet, rifle butt, or boot,

I don't give a fock! Cos mark my words, now, he'll give *ye* no quarter, so he won't! Ach, we'll be grand, boys, so we will! Last man up that fockin' wee hill buys the pints in *The Crown* when we get back to Belfast!'

As a wave of nervous laughter ripples across 'B' Company, Andy takes a neatly folded Orange Sash from his pocket and puts it on solemnly and deliberately. A big, burly Lewis gunner also dons his Sash, as do a number of the other men.

Andy offers Tommy his hand. 'Good luck, Tommy lad!'

Tommy pumps the veteran Serjeant's hand, smiling. 'Best o' luck, Andy! See ye in *The Crown!*'

Andy moves on to Billy, who can't help staring for a moment at Andy's Sash. 'Good luck to ye now, Billy! Yer a good man, so y'are. A real fighter! Give 'em hell, now, lad!'

Billy, emotional, swallows hard. '*I will*, Sarn't!'

Andy leans closer to Billy, still clasping his hand, lowering his voice to an urgent whisper. 'Make sure an' keep an eye on yer mucker Nelson now, lad.'

'I'll not be leavin' his side, Sarn't! Good luck to ye now, *Andy*. See ye in *The Crown.*'

'Aye, lad.' Andy gives Billy a parting clap on the shoulder and with a final nod moves on to Davey, grasping him by the hand. 'Are ye well, Mr. Patterson?' he enquires cheerfully, as if they might have been two passing gentlemen greeting each other while out for a stroll of an early Summer's morning on Donegall Place.

'Aye, fine thank ye Sarn't', Davey replies nervously.

'Well, good luck to ye now, lad! Ach, ye'll be grand, Davey, so ye will! Just follow me, Nelson and McNally when it all kicks off. Your brother Norman would be proud of ye, so he would, God rest him.'

Davey swallows hard. 'Thank ye, Sarn't, and the best o' luck to ye!'

Andy makes his way further on down the trench, shaking hands with the other men of 'B' Company, wishing them luck, offering them an encouraging word, bidding them farewell.

Tommy tentatively offers Davey his hand. 'Best of luck, Davey? No hard feelin's, mate, eh?'

Davey takes Tommy's hand with a grin and pumps it vigorously. 'No hard feelin's, Tommy. I think ye actually bate some fockin' sense into me mate, so ye did!'

'Aye, well', replies Tommy with a short laugh, 'Any time ye're in need of *another* good fockin' lampin', Patterson, let me know!'

The two young men burst out laughing. 'Fock ye very much, Nelson! Fock ye and good luck!'

Tommy Nelson and Billy McNally face each other silently for a moment before shaking hands and embracing warmly. Billy regards his friend anxiously, his voice hushed with emotion. 'Tommy, I just want to ye to know that *ye are my brother* – the only brother I've ever known, or ever *will* ever know. I'll be beside ye all the way mate, so I will, *no matter what*.' Billy forces a wan smile. 'Sher it'll all be over in a flash, so it will, and we'll be back to Belfast before we know it. Just keep thinkin' about Mary, Tommy. Think about gettin' back to Mary.' He winks at his friend. 'I've a Best Man's speech to be workin' on, ye know.'

Tommy exhales a long, shaky breath. 'Thanks, mate. Ye are my brother too, Billy... *Always*. Aye, and I'll be with ye too, mate! *Every bloody step o' the way!* Good luck and God Bless.' Tommy turns away for a moment, emotion threatening to overwhelm him.

A visibly moved Davey Patterson pauses, affording the two friends their moment, before offering his hand to Billy again. 'Good luck, McNally! See ye in *The Crown?'*

Billy manages a mischievous grin. 'Aye! And the pints'll be on *ye*, ya wee shite, ya!'

Suddenly, Captain McAllister re-appears, striding down the trench among the saluting men, returning their courtesies distractedly. 'Righto lads, what about ye?' He checks his watch. 'We'll be movin' out into No Man's Land in a minute. When we go, keep down and keep quiet 'til ye hear me blow the whistle. Then get up that wee hill as quick as ye can, now. Keep movin' forward *no matter what!* Stop for *nothin'* and stop for *no-one!'*

McAllister clears his throat a little self-consciously. 'Now before we go lads, I just want to say a few words to ye all...' As the men of 'B' Company look on in expectant silence, Captain McAllister, appearing to heed for the first time the men that have donned their Sashes, produces an orange handkerchief and knots it into an armband, slipping it up his left arm. He straightens himself up, regarding the men intently, raising his voice to be heard over the never-ending thunder of the barrage.

'Here we stand, as proud a host of Ulstermen as ever I've seen, on the morning of the two hundredth and twenty-sixth anniversary of the Battle of the Boyne! What a magnificent victory it was for King William and our people, over tyranny! That momentous victory ensured the birth of modern democracy and guaranteed civil and religious liberty for *all!* Now, here we stand, my fellow Ulstermen, ready to do our duty once again for God and Ulster!'

There is a terrific cheer from the men and, after a few moments, McAllister raises a quieting hand and points up towards the Schwaben Redoubt. 'Here we face a foe unparalleled in numbers, or in savagery, in the history of warfare! He is well-armed, well-trained, and well dug-in! But he is *not* prepared to withstand an attack from a force such as *this!* Ye are *all* volunteers, *to a man!* The bravest of the brave! The flower of our beloved Ulster! *No* enemy could withstand so magnificent a force such as I now see before me here today, on this glorious, historic, First of July morning! Ye are without doubt the finest body of men I have ever had the privilege to command! I am proud of ye *all*, boys! God save Ulster! God save the King! Three cheers for King George! *Hip, hip!'*

'HOORAY!'

'Hip, hip!'

'HOORAY!'

'Hip, hip!'

'HOORAY!'

'Now, *do* yer duty, men! Make Ulster proud! *NO SURRENDER!'*

'NO SURRENDER!'

The roar of the artillery is almost surpassed by the volume of the cheer that erupts from the men. Captain McAllister glances at his watch again. 'Sarn't McNair! Give the men the order to fix bayonets, if ye please!'

Andy salutes. 'Very good, Sir!' Exhilarated, he draws in a deep breath.

'BAYONETS!'

There is a harsh rasping of steel on leather as the men draw their bayonets as one. A forest of wickedly glinting steel springs up as they hold the bayonets aloft.

'BAYONETS, FIX!'

There is a volley of metallic clicks as each man fixes eighteen inches of sharpened cold steel to his Lee-Enfield rifle. McAllister checks the time again, the hands of his watch showing exactly oh-seven-ten hours. 'Righto, lads! Move out!' he commands, without taking his eyes off his watch.

Andy motions the men towards the entrance to the Russian Sap, snaking grimly out into No Man's Land. 'Come on, move it out, now, boys! Let's go! Smartly, now!'

The men gradually disappear down the Sap as the Royal Artillery continues to pound the German positions mercilessly. Captain McAllister is the last man to go down the Sap. He looks around somewhat uneasily at the now-deserted trench, gripped suddenly by an eerie, almost ghostly sensation. *My God, it's already like we were never here.*

CHAPTER TEN

Somme, 1ˢᵗ July, 1916

The men of the Ulster Division line the Sap, waiting tensely as the volume and intensity of the British artillery barrage reaches a terrifying, apocalyptic crescendo. The men regard each other nervously as suddenly, the very earth beneath their feet begins to tremble, as if in protest at the abuses heaped upon it at the hands of men. There is a massive explosion to the north of their position as forty thousand pounds of ammonal in the mine under Hawthorn Ridge is detonated, heaving countless tons of earth, and the body parts of unfortunate German defenders high into the air.

Tommy and Billy exchange knowing glances. *Bob.* Tommy imagines the wiry little Canadian burrowing doggedly through the blue clay somewhere a hundred feet under the Messines Ridge in Flanders, and smiles grimly to himself. *I wonder did ye feel that, Bob McKnight, wherever ye are?*

Some minutes later there is an even bigger detonation, this time to the south-east of them, in the direction of La Boiselle. The men look on in awe as a plume of smoke and earth soars thousands of feet into the air, launched skywards by a geyser of fire that seems to erupt from the very bowels of the earth itself. A feeling of unreality washes over Billy, and he closes his eyes for a moment. *Oh God, it's like the end of the world.*

Captain McAllister licks his lips nervously and checks his watch again as the artillery barrage gradually ceases until all is eerily, deathly quiet. The hands of his watch show exactly zero-seven-thirty hours. Tommy looks up incredulously as somewhere high over No Man's Land, a lark begins to sing.

McAllister draws his revolver. 'Righto lads, here we go! This is it! Good luck to ye all!' He raises his whistle to his lips with a slightly trembling hand and blows three long blasts, rising up out of the Sap and beckoning his men to follow him. The distant sounds of whistles blowing can be heard all along the British line. The men of the 36th (Ulster) Division rise up into history.

'Remember the Boyne, lads!'

'For God and Ulster!'

'No Surrender!'

'NO SURRENDER!'

For a few moments, the war-cries of thousands of men unite into a solid, furious wall of noise as they begin the charge. Through the haze of smoke still obscuring the enemy lines, Andy can faintly but clearly hear commands being shouted in German, and the unmistakeable oily, metallic clicks of weapons being cocked. His blood freezes. *Ah, Jesus.*

A sinister, silent volley of flashes twinkles through the haze, and suddenly the air is alive with zinging, hissing metal and the sickening wet thuds of bullets smacking into flesh, lazily followed by the staccato rattle of machine-gun fire and single rifle shots from the German lines.

Ulstermen fall in little puffs of bloody mist as the German Maxims, firing in short bursts, scythe through them like rows of corn. Wounded men begin to scream in a piteous chorus of agony. The big Lewis gunner, his eyes wide with fury and terror in equal measure, roars and begins to fire his machine-gun from the hip as he advances.

The men quicken their pace as they press onwards towards the German lines, advancing hunched over with their heads down, as if charging into the teeth of a gale – a murderous gale of lead.

A sniper's bullet hisses through Captain McAllister's shoulder, impacting and exiting his body with a misty red puff, staggering him. The shocked officer looks numbly down at the bloody wound in his shoulder, clasping a shaking hand to it as he sinks to the ground. 'Oh Jesus, I'm hit! I'm hit, so I am! Stretcher bearers! S-stretcher... b-bear... ers...'

ZING-ZING! As he begins to lose consciousness, two more rounds in quick succession smack into McAllister with sickening meaty thuds as he lies on the ground, the first bullet hitting him in the thigh, the second hitting him in the chest, killing him instantly.

Davey, his heart pounding, his eyes wide with terror, half-runs, half-shambles past the officer's body. *Jesus, lads, the Rupert's copped it, so he has!'*

Andy grits his teeth as he advances through the hail of lead. *'B' COMPANY! ON ME! ON ME! LET'S GO! C'MON, GET UP THAT FOCKIN' HILL!'*

The men begin to rally to the veteran Serjeant as the withering storm of fire from the German lines continues to thin their ranks still further. German artillery salvos now begin to land among the Ulstermen, adding to the chaos and the slaughter. The big Lewis gunner, advancing just ahead of Billy and still firing his machine-gun from the hip, takes a direct hit from a 10.5 centimetre shell, which literally vaporises him. When Billy, momentarily blinded by the explosion, looks back to where the Lewis gunner once stood, there is nothing left save for a small, smoking crater. A jumble of body parts, twisted metal and smouldering pieces of Orange Sash rain down upon Billy. He flinches numbly as a charred human hand bounces off his helmet with a loud, metallic *BOINK,* landing on the ground in front of him in a grotesque parody of the emblem of Ulster.

Sobbing now, Billy continues to shamble onwards, passing a tall, vaguely familiar figure lying on his back, his muck-covered entrails lying in a foul, steaming pile beside him in the dirt. McEntaggart moans, making feeble attempts to stuff his own innards back into his shattered body. Blood gushes from the dying man's mouth as looks up and cries out to Billy piteously. *'Help me! For the love of Jesus, PLEASE HELP ME!'*

Billy begins to hyperventilate, looking around to make sure that Tommy, Andy and Davey are still beside him. Breathlessly, he begins to murmur a prayer. 'Hail Mary - '

Andy still bravely urges the survivors forward. *'C'MON! KEEP GOIN' BOYS! DON'T BUNCH UP, NOW!'* A three-round burst of machine-gun fire stitches across his stomach, felling him in a bloody haze. Lying on his back, Andy clutches a shaking hand to his spurting, eviscerated belly. More shots crack out from the Schwaben Redoubt, kicking up angry puffs of earth around him.

His belly afire, Andy clenches his teeth through the agony. An ominous coldness begins to spread upwards from his legs.

'B- B- Bastards!'

' - Full of Grace - '

Davey cries out in despair. 'Shite! *No!* Sarn't McNair's hit! He's down!'

' - The Lord is with Thee - '

'Bastards! *BASTARDS!*' Tommy urges the men on, his eyes wild with fury. '*KEEP FOCKIN' GOIN'!*'

NO! Andy feels death begin to cover him like a soft, dark blanket, and sobbingly fights it tooth and nail. 'I'm cold, lads... I'm so c- c- cold... Jesus, I can't see! *I CAN'T SEE!*' He finally begins to let go as he feels a blessed warmth envelope him.

Ma.

No more cold.

'Ma...'

Blissful peace. Andy McNair's last breath comes out in a long, almost contented sigh.

Another German shell explodes nearby, tossing three Ulstermen into the air like bloody, broken toys. Volleys of rifle fire and controlled, short bursts from the Maxims continue to crackle down from the German lines, yet still the Ulstermen charge on.

' - Blessed Art Thou amongst women, and blessed is the fruit of Thy Womb - '

ZINGTHOCK! A sniper's bullet catches Davey high in the chest, the dum-dum round blowing half his back away in a bloody spatter.

' - JESUS! - '

DAVEY falls to the ground, his breath coming hard in great, wheezing gasps. He cries out with the last of his strength. 'BILLY!'

'Davey! NO!' His eyes rolling in horror, Billy turns to rush to the dying young man's side, when he feels Tommy's restraining hand on his shoulder. He whirls around angrily to his friend as bullets begin to kick up puffs of dirt around them, perilously close.

Gripping his friend's arm, Tommy shouts to be heard above the din of battle. 'Don't stop, mate! Don't stop or we're as good as dead! I'm sorry, mate, Davey's gone! HE'S GONE! Keep goin' Billy!

We're nearly there, mate! C'mon! LET'S GO AND CLEAN THESE FOCKERS OUT!'

I'm sorry, Davey. Choking back a sob as he looks around one last time at the dying young man, Billy allows himself to be led forward again by Tommy, the two men shambling up a steep rise towards the parapet of the German trench.

Davey feels the life ebbing from him with every faltering beat of his heart, his blood soaking slowly into the chalky soil of the Somme. He becomes suddenly calm, floating above the pain.

Norman, wait for me...

ZINGTHOCK! A second bullet smacks into the meat of his thigh unheeded, his dying body now beyond feeling such things.

Daddy...

A single tear courses down the side of his grey, dirt-streaked face as he remembers his father's letter. He closes his eyes and tries to speak, his voice a mere choking, faltering whisper.

'The Lord is my Shepherd; I shall not - '

ZINGTHOCK! Davey's last prayer remains unfinished as another sniper's bullet takes the top of his head away in a red spray.

Tommy and Billy dive for cover just short of the German line as a Maxim opens up directly above them, loosing off a short burst into No Man's Land. They land breathlessly in a shell-hole and lie there for a moment, chests heaving. Wide-eyed, wild-eyed, they cling to one another in a brief moment of triumph, exulting in each other's survival.

The intensity of the defensive fire begins to slacken noticeably as Ulstermen begin to reach the German lines and infiltrate their positions. Tommy and Billy listen to the distant sounds of steel slicing mercilessly through flesh and the pitiful screams as their comrades vent their fury on the German defenders.

The machine-gun above them looses off another three-round burst. They hear an order being given in German, followed by another short burst from the Maxim.

Tommy takes a deep breath and rests his hand on Billy's heaving shoulder. 'Right mate, let's use our bombs. We'll wait for their next burst, give them a bomb each straight after, and then we'll follow up with the bayonet! Okay?'

Billy nods breathlessly. 'Ready, mate!'

They pull the pins from their grenades and wait for a few moments in tense silence. After the next burst from the Maxim, Tommy and Billy rise up and lob their grenades up over the parapet, then crouch back down in the shell-hole for cover. The German soldiers' horrified exclamations are cut short by two loud blasts as the grenades detonate.

Tommy and Billy are up roaring over the parapet in an instant. They jump into the trench either side of the machine-gun nest, ready with their bayonets, but their grenades have done their job. The smoking, tattered corpses of three young German soldiers lie in a bloody grey heap around their mangled machine-gun. The position appears otherwise deserted, and the two Ulstermen begin to advance cautiously down the trench, bayonets at the ready.

A single shot rings out from behind them, the bullet thudding into Billy's back and exiting his chest in a misty red spatter. Tommy, paralysed by shock, can only look on in horror as Billy staggers against the wall of the trench, sliding bloodily down it until he sits on the duckboards, his face turning ashen. Billy looks down in confusion at the spreading rosette of claret on the front of his tunic, then up at the shocked face of his friend. *'Tommy'* is all he manages to whisper as he dies.

Tommy, beginning to recover his senses, turns around to face Billy's killer, a terrified-looking sixteen-year-old German boy whose hands are trembling so badly that he is unable to pull back the bolt of his rifle to chamber another round. Snarling, Tommy charges at the young soldier, who throws his rifle on the ground and falls to his knees with his hands raised, his whole body shaking with terror.

'K- *Kamerad! Ich gebe auf!*'

Tommy, mad with grief, rage, and the bloodlust of battle, stands over the boy, readying a bayonet thrust. The young German puts his hands together in a gesture of supplication, his eyes wild with terror.

'Ich gebe auf! *Bitte!*'

He's just a scared fockin' wee boy. Tommy suddenly looks uncertain, his poised bayonet wavering slightly. He glances away for a moment, unable to look at the young soldier kneeling tearfully in front of him, his mind a whirl of confusion. He sees Billy's body and turns around again angrily as the boy continues to plead for his life.

'*Shut yer fockin' hole ya wee bastard, ye!*'

He hears Andy's voice in his head.

And when we get to the top up there, fockin' give it to 'im with whatever ye have! Bayonet, bullet, rifle butt, or boot, I don't give a fock! Cos mark my words, now, he'll give ye no quarter, so he won't!

The young soldier's pitiful entreaties fade to an unheeded mumble as a series of old memories of Billy flashes briefly through Tommy's whirling mind -

The two of them about eight years old, walking down the red-brick terraces of Bluebell Avenue, laughing as a five-year-old Mary skips between them, holding their hands and looking adoringly up at both of them.

Standing back-to-back at the end of Bluebell Avenue, taking on the Murphy boys and the Bell boys together in a wild melee.

Walking down Bluebell Avenue with their fathers towards the shipyard, chatting and laughing as they go. The massive hull of the RMS Titanic, under construction and covered in scaffolding, is visible in the distance, towering above the red-brick terraces of East Belfast.

As he still holds the rifle ready for a bayonet thrust in trembling hands, Tommy hears Billy's voice in his head.

Tommy, I just want to ye to know that ye are my brother – the only brother I've ever known, or ever will know. I'll be beside ye all the way mate, so I will, no matter what.

Tommy looks back again at his friend's body and his face hardens. He whirls on the still-pleading German boy and thrusts his bayonet. Eighteen inches of steel enters through the young soldier's mouth with a sickening, bloody rasp, breaking teeth and cutting the boy's speech off in mid-sentence to a wet, choking gurgle. It exits the back of his neck with a gristly crunch, the boy's body twitching obscenely until Tommy withdraws the bayonet with a wet, bloody scrape and the young soldier's corpse falls limply to the ground.

Tommy looks down at the ruined face of the young German soldier and remembers his own words to Davey in the trench:

We're all God's children, Patterson, ye know.

Tommy's face crumples and his breath comes out in a long, choking sob. He staggers over to the wall of the trench and begins to retch, heedless of the German officer quietly rounding the corner barely twenty feet behind him, his Mauser pistol raised.

The German officer fires twice into Tommy's back, then falls in a bloody mist as a brace of shots strike him in the chest in quick succession, fired by two Ulstermen who have just gained the top of the parapet. They jump down into the trench, landing heavily on the duckboards, and raise their rifles cautiously, taking stock of the bloody scene around them.

'C'mon, Sammy let's go left! I'll bet that focker came up from a bunker somewhere around the corner!'

They hasten on down the trench, leaping over the body of the German officer, and disappear around the corner from whence he came. The sound of their boots pounding on the duckboards begins to fade.

Tommy faintly hears their voices drifting back to him, as if from a huge distance away.

'Come out ye fockers!'

'Bastards!'

Tommy hears the distant report of a rifle, then everything begins to fade - sounds, colours, even light itself. Groaning, Tommy desperately begins to crawl back towards the body of his friend before the approaching darkness can overhaul him. He stops for a moment, his body wracked by pain, and coughs up a dark glut of blood. *Ah, Jesus.*

Billy, Mary, I'm sorry...

He begins to crawl again, eventually reaching the spot where Billy sits against the wall of the trench, his head slumped on his chest. With a supreme, groaning effort, Tommy manages to prop himself up beside the body of his dead friend. A single tear rolls down his pale cheek as he reaches across and closes Billy's eyes, his hand lingering for a moment in a last farewell to his friend.

As his sight begins to fade, Tommy manages to take his photograph of Mary from his pocket. He traces a shaking finger down Mary's smiling face, then closes his eyes. Tommy's head slumps against Billy's shoulder as the photograph falls from his fingers and lands on the ground between them.

Oh Mary, my love...

Somewhere, high over the battlefield, a lark begins to sing.

CHAPTER ELEVEN

Belfast, July 1916

The telegrams descend on the households of Ulster like a biblical plague. In Bluebell Avenue, Mary and Iris are mercifully alone in the house, Dougie having by now joined his father at the shipyard. The women exchange a look of dread as they hear an ominous knocking at the front door. Iris Nelson rises stiffly from the kitchen table and walks slowly, reluctantly up the hall.

Mary hears her mother begin to scream from across the street and knows that her brother is dead.

Billy! She can only repeat his name over and over in her mind, as if it were an invocation that might somehow bring him back. Numbly, she feels her body fill with a black inertia, the grief and dread rising inside her like a dark, evil liquid.

Mary's hand flies trembling to her mouth as panic suddenly threatens to overwhelm her.

Oh God, please... No! Please spare me Tommy! Please spare Tommy for our baby!

But there is to be no Passover this morning in Bluebell Avenue. Iris Nelson shuffles her way back into the kitchen holding a telegram, her face a frozen mask of unspeakable sorrow. With a sob of pure despair, Mary flies to her. The women cling desperately to each other as the dam of their grief finally bursts and their cries join a chorus of lament that rises up all over Belfast, from the Newtownards Road to the Shankill, from Sandy Row to Tiger's Bay.

Few are spared.

CHAPTER TWELVE

Belfast, July 1916

The letter is pushed hastily through the Nelson's letterbox a week later. Mary can hear her mother's footsteps retreating slowly back across Bluebell Avenue, and feels a stab of pity for her which she can't quite manage to crush. *She's lost a daughter and her only son... But her daughter by choice.*

Brigid McNally has had no contact with Mary since the day she told her to leave her house and, moreover, has also completely avoided Iris and George Nelson. Mary is sure that her mother would have taken a lesser woman to task for having the temerity to take in her fallen daughter, right under her nose across the street no less, but knows better than to try anything on with Iris.

Life among the men goes on much as before, with George Nelson and Mick McNally still on friendly terms. They still walk to and from the Shipyard together, albeit now sharing the bond of silent grief, which somehow pulls them even closer to each other like some dark, inexorable knot. These days they are accompanied by the equally forlorn figure of Dougie, heartbroken after the loss of his big brother, his hero. Dougie tells his father that he wants to join up - for Tommy - but understandably, George and Iris Nelson will have none of it, telling him that he is too young, that the Nelsons have sacrificed enough, and that it is the very last thing in the world that his big brother would want for him. It silences Dougie - for now.

George Nelson tells Mary that her father has tried to speak to his wife about taking Mary back, but without success. Mick McNally tells him sadly that in fact Billy's death only seems to have hardened her heart further, if anything.

It'll be alright though, she'll come around in time, lass – ye'll see! George keeps assuring her. Mary is doubtful, yet grateful for the big man's compassion, and likes him for the kind-hearted soul that he is - as kind-hearted in his own rough, quiet way as his remarkable wife, Iris.

The envelope is addressed to Miss Mary McNally, 8 Bluebell Avenue, Belfast, in Tommy's handwriting. Mary can only stare numbly at the envelope for a long time, unable to open it, as if the very act will serve but to reinforce the finality, the irrevocability of Tommy's loss.

Mary lets out a long sigh as she somehow summons to the courage to read Tommy's last letter.

2417 Rifleman Thos. Nelson,

B Coy., - Battalion,

Royal Irish Rifles,

Thiepval Wood,

Somme,

France.

Friday, 30ᵗʰ June 1916

Miss Mary McNally,

8 Bluebell Avenue,

Belfast.

My Darling Mary,

I finally received your letter this evening, my love. We are, at the moment, entrenched in what was once Thiepval Wood, awaiting the off early tomorrow morning. It is good a thing, I believe, that your letter arrived when it did, for it leaves me with little time to brood over matters before we must go over the top.

I can only tell you what joy and comfort your words brought me, my darling. Please know that because of you, my mind is calm and at peace, and your love gives me the grace and strength to face what I know must come tomorrow. I also take comfort in the knowledge that I will not be facing the ordeal alone, but that Billy and I will side by side, as always, along with the other good men here.

I write this letter crouched in a trench looking at your smiling face, my love, knowing that these may be my last words to you. We have been told that it will be a walkover for us tomorrow, that our artillery will have obliterated the German positions, but not a man here believes it, not even the most gung-ho of our officers. Nevertheless, we are all determined to do our duty, and do it well.

I hope to see your dear face again soon, my darling Mary, and to hold you in my arms. I can think of nothing else. However, if it is to be my fate not to return to you my love, please know that you are, have always been and always will be forever in my heart, and that I will always be by your side. Please give my love to Siobhán and Deirdre, and to your mother and father also. Farewell for now, my love.

Yours always,

Tommy.

She goes to their special place one last time, to say goodbye. Mary is, on this occasion, accompanied and assisted by Iris, as her condition now dictates. Eventually, they gain the summit of Cavehill and Mary stands once more looking over the city, crying silent tears, her long hair blowing gently in the breeze. Iris Nelson stands back from her a little, affording Mary her private moment. Mary takes her engagement ring off her necklace and kisses it before slipping it on her finger. Putting her right hand protectively on her belly, now gently blossoming with new life, Mary bows her head in sorrow.

Dear Baby, how I love you so! You are my whole world, my little one. You are all that I have left of my darling Tommy, and Mammy is going to be strong now for us both!

She remembers the words of the last letter that she wrote to Tommy, from this very spot.

Sometimes, when I am lonely, I come up here by myself and I look down upon dear old Belfast, and I think of you. I think of you standing here beside me, my love, and I can almost FEEL the touch of your hand in mine! Please know that I will always love you, my dearest Tommy, and know that I will always be here for you. I would wait for you until the end of time, my darling.

Mary feels the reassuring hand of Iris Nelson on her shoulder.

Goodbye Tommy, my love. Do not be worried, for we are no longer alone. All will be well with us, my dearest Tommy, and I shall tell our dear baby everything about you.

Rest in Peace, my darling.

CHAPTER THIRTEEN

Somme, July 2017

A lark sings merrily in the blue sky as John and Paddy make their way from Thiepval Wood to the cemetery, each of them carrying a poppy wreath. Paddy, abroad for the first time, takes in everything with quiet, wide-eyed wonderment. John Nelson, also on his first visit to the Somme, believes it is the most beautiful, most peaceful place he has ever seen.

Visitors to the immaculately tended cemetery walk respectfully among the neat rows of headstones. A lean and tanned soldier of the Royal Irish Regiment, wearing his caubeen with the green hackle and holding a fife, stands before a grave in silent contemplation.

'There they are, Paddy'. They reach a quiet corner of the cemetery where four headstones stand together under the shade of a maple tree. A lump of emotion gathers in John Nelson's throat for a Grandfather he never knew.

Ah, Grandad, so young…

John puts his arm around Paddy's shoulder as they read the inscriptions on the headstones.

2417 RIFLEMAN THOMAS NELSON

ROYAL IRISH RIFLES

1ST JULY 1916

AGED 22 YEARS

GREATER LOVE HATH NO MAN THAN THIS

2418 RIFLEMAN WILLIAM McNALLY

ROYAL IRISH RIFLES

1ST JULY 1916

AGED 22 YEARS

A DEVOTED SON, A LOVING BROTHER, A LOYAL FRIEND

1572 SERJEANT ANDREW McNAIR

ROYAL IRISH RIFLES

1ST JULY 1916

AGED 43 YEARS

IN ANSWER TO HIS COUNTRY'S CALL HE GAVE HIS
BEST, HIS LIFE, HIS ALL

3129 RIFLEMAN DAVID PATTERSON

ROYAL IRISH RIFLES

1ST JULY 1916

AGED 19 YEARS

PEACE PERFECT PEACE

Unprompted, Paddy steps forward and carefully places his wreath against Tommy's headstone. John follows his Grandson's lead, solemnly placing his wreath against Billy's headstone. He rises slowly and puts his arm around Paddy again.

John looks up and out over the sun-drenched, rolling landscape of the Somme, his voice thick with emotion.

> *'They shall grow not old, as we that are left grow old:*
> *Age shall not weary them, nor the years condemn.*
> *At the going down of the sun and in the morning,*
> *We will remember them.'*

Paddy looks up at his Grandfather, bravely trying to smile through his tears, and manages a whisper. *'We will remember them.'*

John looks down at his Grandson, his heart bursting with love for the boy. Behind them, in the middle of the cemetery, the lone soldier raises his fife to his lips and slowly, hauntingly, begins to play *Abide With Me,* the melody momentarily seeming to still everything, even the birdsong. John looks up into the cloudless blue sky and closes his eyes, peace descending upon him like the soft caress of a warm July breeze.

Rest easy Philip, son. Paddy will be alright. I promise I'll never leave the lad's side as long as I am alive.

Peace, perfect peace.

THE END

ABOUT THE AUTHOR

Peter Keating lives with his family in North County Cork, Ireland – a librarian by day and a writer, performer and artist by night.

24704600R00085

Printed in Great Britain
by Amazon